Downers Grove Public Library
1050 Curtiss St.
Downers Grove, IL 60515
(630) 960-1200
www.downersgrovelibrary.org

GAYLORD

COMPULSION

Also by Heidi Ayarbe

FREEZE FRAME

COMPROMISED

COMPULS1ON

HEIDI AYARBE

BALZER + BRAY

An Imprint of HarperCollins*Publishers*

Balzer + Bray is an imprint of HarperCollins Publishers.

Compulsion
Copyright © 2011 by Heidi Ayarbe
All rights reserved. Printed in the United States of America.
No part of this book may be used or reproduced in any manner whatsoever
without written permission except in the case of brief quotations embodied in
critical articles and reviews. For information address
HarperCollins Children's Books, a division of HarperCollins Publishers,
10 East 53rd Street, New York, NY 10022.
www.harperteen.com

Library of Congress Cataloging-in-Publication Data
Ayarbe, Heidi.
Compulsion / Heidi Ayarbe. — 1st ed.
    p.   cm.
Summary: Poised to lead his high school soccer team to its third straight
state championship, seventeen-year-old star player Jake Martin struggles to keep
hidden his nearly debilitating obsessive-compulsive disorder.
ISBN 978-0-06-199386-2 (trade bdg.)
    [1. Soccer—Fiction. 2. Obsessive-compulsive disorder—Fiction. 3.
Emotional problems—Fiction. 4. Interpersonal relations—Fiction. 5. High
schools—Fiction. 6. Schools—Fiction.]   I. Title.
PZ7.A9618Con   2011   2010027826
[Fic]—dc22   CIP
                                                                          AC

Typography by Jennifer Rozbruch
11 12 13 14 15   CG/RRDB   10 9 8 7 6 5 4 3 2 1
❖
First Edition

For Lisa, her strength and courage.
This is also for Amelia, whose laughter fills my world.
And always, Cesar.

Wednesday, 6:13 p.m.

TWO THE SPIDERS RETURN

Tanya Reese's Tinker Bell tattoo flits on her pale shoulder, blowing on a dandelion, its fluff spiraling down her back. Tanya shivers. It's November and she's wearing an off-the-shoulder shirt. Mom would say, "Not weather appropriate." I don't offer her my jacket because I'm not a fucking Boy Scout and would rather stare at the goose-bumped flesh and imagine where the trail of wispy dandelion seeds might lead me. *Blow hard and make a wish.*

"Cap'n Hook, eyes up front," Luc says and laughs. "Jake. Cash?" He holds out his hand.

I tear my eyes from Tanya's shoulder and pull out my wallet, only to find a limp Lincoln and taped-together Washington.

Luc raises his eyebrows.

I pat the money in my front pocket—the cash Dad gave me to pay Mr. Hartman. "C'mon, asshole," Luc says. Tanya and Amy giggle. Tanya opens her purse. "I've got money too."

I shake my head. "No. That's okay. I got it." I take out Dad's money and hand it to the zitty kid behind the cash register. "My treat tonight."

Okay. Dad's treat. No big deal.

The register chimes and the drawer slides closed. "Thanks for coming to In-N-Out." He hands me my change, and I shove it into my pocket before counting it but can't help fingering the bills and coins—four bills, seven coins. *Eleven. OK.*

Luc puts his wallet away. "Nice, Martin," and hands me the tray of food. Tanya smiles, and I follow her milk-white skin to the booth.

The four of us cram into the vinyl-and-Formica fast-food heaven, the tray piled high with burgers, fries, and shakes. We have everything, including hot chicks, to make for a perfect culinary experience. I glance at Tanya as she picks up a french fry, bites, then double dips it in the runny, room-temp ketchup. Blue nails. Red ketchup. Double dipping.

"What's up?" she asks.

I'm such a fuck, all I can say is "Your nails. They're,

um . . . blue." And then the smells hit me: grease, pine floor polish, doused-on cologne from Carson High's soccer team, and—I sniff in deep—a faint smell of curdled milk. I look back and some mom has a baby draped over her shoulder, white chunky milk running down the baby's chin.

I inhale and gag, then try to exhale the stink from my nostrils, sure the hair has trapped the odors. When I open my mouth to gasp for air, the stench is palpable—something I could spoon up into a bowl and eat—so I slam my mouth shut. I feel sweat trickle down my back—pooling on my tailbone. I hold my breath to try to make everything black. Black is better than the gray of the webs that I feel creeping up my neck. Way better.

Tanya scoots closer, her shoulder nestled against my chest. The Tinker Bell tattoo stretches across her right shoulder blade when Tanya reaches across the table—Tink's smile turning into a distorted Munch-like grimace. "Well, yeah," she says. "We are in Spirit Week . . . for *you* guys." She laughs, then slips her hand in mine—soft hands with slick fingertips and blue nails.

Tick-tock, tick-tock, tick-tock —Captain Hook only had to worry about Tock. My crocodile is fucking everywhere.

I feel the familiar itch. *Not. This. Week.* I think about the game, the team.

I grasp onto my watch—looking at the time. I have to count. Maybe just today.

I need the magic.

The team needs the magic. This is for them.

6:14 p.m.

Six fourteen. Six plus one is seven plus four is eleven. OK.

I have exactly forty-five minutes and thirty-two, thirty-one—less than forty-six minutes to get to Hartman's, pick up the meat for Dad, and get home. Plenty of time.

Not plenty of cash.

Fuck.

Fuck.

I down my Flying Dutchman and a Neapolitan shake; I'm still hungry but blew everything I couldn't spare on food Tanya won't eat. The entire Carson High soccer team has come—team tradition—slurping down shakes and ingesting burgers at alarming speed.

Tanya and Amy shouldn't even be here to begin with. No other chicks are.

But Luc's the captain. He can bring anybody.

And I'm Magic Martin.

My stomach growls. I lean back in the booth wondering what Mom made for dinner.

"Goddamn, Martin, why don't you show some manners, man? Breathe between bites at least."

I shrug. "I was hungry." I swallow down a belch. That's about as gentlemanly as they'll get tonight. I try to stretch, but Tanya has crammed me into the booth.

She giggles. "I can't *believe* you eat that much." Her fingers are wrapped around the burger, tipped with those chipped blue nails. She takes one of those dainty-chick bites. I've always told Kasey to not do that when she starts going out. Eat like a real person, not some kind of chicken pecking at corn. Luckily Kase eats a lot as long as nothing on her plate is touching. That drives her nuts.

The tingling in the back of my neck begins to sting—like jellyfish tentacles. It's not a big deal. I'll get through the rest of dinner. I just have to focus. I look at the clock hanging on the wall.

6:26

The clock on the wall isn't in time to my watch. I look at the hands of my watch and count the seconds.

Four seconds faster than the clock.

So right now it's 6:26 and 6:27—for four seconds.

Four. Fuck.

My resting heart rate is forty-seven beats per minute.

I feel my pulse and watch the seconds on the clock. Sixty-three.

Just relax.

Six plus two is eight plus six is fourteen minus two is twelve minus six is six. Fuck. Plus two is eight...

Numbers blur. Sweat stings my eyes.

Inhale.

Exhale.

6:28

Six twenty-eight. The numbers spin. I look across at Luc, but he's too busy trying to cop a feel of Amy to give a shit what's going on. A filthy film of grease coats the glass on the clock on the wall.

I pull my eyes from the clock and count the fries in the bag. *Thirteen.* Tanya eats another, *twelve,* and another and another until there are only four left. Then she tries to give me one, but I jerk my head back. "No thanks, um. Just . . . "

Numbers, just look at the numbers. But I can't because my watch and the clock aren't in sync and the numbers won't work that way.

Sweat drips down my temple, tickling my chin. I lean my head down, feeling the perspiration, wiping it with a napkin.

It's like something clicks in my brain, waking up things that should be left to sleep. One by one neurons come to life, sizzling and charring the only good connections that are left, turning my brain into a smoke-filled frazzle. And I can feel the familiar tickle of spider legs crawling up my spine.

I scratch at the back of my neck. I haven't felt this for a while.

Maybe a couple of weeks. It's been a good two weeks.
Fuck.

"This Saturday is going to be magic," Tanya says.

Magic.

For a second I can imagine the game, bring my mind to Saturday and erase this moment, the smells, the sounds, and the freak Tinker Bell tattoo. Magic.

Tick-tock, tick-tock.

Luc leans back in the booth, his arms crossed behind his head. "Saturday's game is everything. You can't imagine," he says to Amy, then looks at me. "Right?"

No. *He* can't imagine. Everything in my life depends on Saturday. I glance at the clock, work out the numbers, and sigh. It won't be long until that's all gone—only, though, if Saturday is magic.

"What do you feel when you get on that field with all those people cheering for you?" Tanya leans in and stares at me intently, those blue polished nails holding that greasy fry, the other hand, a shriveled husk of dried skin and bone, in mine. Tinker Bell's fairy dust looks like flecks of mustard-colored sewage splatter, her head deformed by Tanya's jutting shoulder bone.

Tanya looks up at me with big brown eyes—giant. I mean alien giant, and a little face that ends in a tiny pointed chin. She wears a black choker around her neck with a heart charm dangling from some silver loops.

I'm struck by the idea that she looks a lot like our neighbor Sarah Merckley's Chihuahua. What's his name? Ramón. Wearing makeup, of course, with blue-painted claws.

Inhale. The curdled milk mixes with Tanya's perfume—some fruity, flowery shit that smells like bathroom potpourri spray.

"Well?" she asks.

"Indescribable," says Luc, scowling at me.

Tanya moves closer, shoving her hipbone against my thigh. I squirm to get space, but she takes it like I'm making more room for her and moves in closer.

Give me some fucking space!

I'm not really speaking. I know this because nobody is looking at me weird.

I try to keep my voice in my head—to work out a way to make my thoughts sound normal. Sane. My heart hammers in my chest, pulsates in my ears, and I can't hear above the clamor. I wipe my sweat-slick palms on my thighs and peel off my sweatshirt.

Just don't breathe.

Through the blur of the webs in my brain, I stare at the french fry dangling like a waterlogged cigarette from Tanya's blue fingertips. If I tried, I could probably make out my reflection in the sheen of grease.

Count.

I look at the time. Subtract, divide, add. Anything to make the numbers prime. Like number roulette in my head, spinning and spinning. I wait for the marble to drop in the slot; I feel my pulse.

Eighty-three.

Spinning, spinning, the marble won't drop and it feels like my head will explode. Now *that* would be a mess for Luc to explain to my family—spontaneous head explosion and brain matter all over In-N-Out.

Tanya's talking. Talking like she eats—little pecks of words suspended in front of us. Nothing of substance. Just peck, peck, peck. I check my pulse.

Eighty-six.

The spiders crawl and they weave, the pain working its way up my spine until it feels like somebody is stabbing my temples with ice picks. Their thick-spun webs cloud everything, making it hard to think.

I count.

I turn away from the clock and look back at the three fries in the bag and the one in Tanya's fingers. All I need her to do is eat the fucking fry. *Just eat it. Just eat the goddamned french fry.*

But she drops it back in the bag. Leaving four. *Four.* Fuck.

"What's wrong with you?" she asks, pulling her hand from mine, looking to Luc for help. My entire back is drenched in sweat; my palm's slicker than her greasy blue-fingered french-fry hands.

Luc flings a limp pickle at me. "Jesus, man. What's with you?"

Inhale.

I count breaths. *One . . . seventeen . . .* inhale, exhale. Their words are muffled by the pounding in my head, and I try to make out what they're saying. Luc absently reaches over and eats a fry from the bag, leaving three.

Exhale.

The spinning slows to a stop, the marble drops into a slot, and the numbers fall into place.

Three. I shake my head and look up at Luc and Amy. Tanya's moved as far from me as possible, sitting at the edge of the booth. Thank God. She moves to pick up another fry and I grab her hand. "Leave the three," I say, and almost feel guilty looking at her untouched burger. Those fries were probably two thirds of her caloric intake for the day.

Luc laughs. Uncomfortable. I've embarrassed him again. I know that he sometimes wishes I was different—like him. "C'mon, man. You've done one too many wind sprints today." He turns to Tanya and Amy. "He's always like this before games." He smiles. "Superstitious," he mouths.

They both nod enthusiastically. That explains it. Explains it all.

"I'm tired," I say. "Real tired."

Fuck.

Luc motions for all of us to stand up, and I peel myself from the booth, leaving an embarrassing wet mark on the vinyl cover. Most of the team is gone. Grundy, Diaz, and

Keller are the last ones hanging around, flick-punting grilled onions over the heads of some girls in the booth in front of them.

My body smells sour; I just want to shower and wash it all away. I sometimes wonder: If I scrub hard enough, will I slip down the drain?

What if . . .

Stop. It.

7:03

Seven-oh-three. Seven plus three is ten. Seven minus three is four.

Fuckfuckfuckfuckfuck.

Tick-tock, tick-tock.

"Yeah. I know. Okayokayokay."

And I realize I'm speaking out loud because Tanya, Amy, and Luc exchange one of those oh-my-god-he's-got-a-boner-and-is-wearing-sweatpants glances. We pile into the car and drive by Hartman's—the windows dark except for the neon glow of the closed sign.

"Sorry, man," Luc says. "I'd have sworn they were open till seven thirty."

The spiders are going mad in my brain, but I can still think clear enough to know Dad's gonna shit when he finds out I didn't pick up the meat and spent his cash on In-N-Out. Things have been better since he was promoted to driver at UPS, but with Mom out of work and on heavy meds, we still don't have much to spare. Shit, I don't even have a letterman's jacket.

"A hard-on is no excuse to flake out on your family responsibilities."

"What are you talking about, *guevón*?" Luc says.

Tanya and Amy laugh a nervous laugh. I force one too, but it sounds real. Easy. "Just trying to imagine the conversation I'm going to have with my dad."

"About a hard-on?" Luc shakes his head. "Those are things you should keep to yourself, man." The car fills with laughter, erasing my ultraweirdness.

I push the thoughts back in where they can't be heard. *Shut up. Just. Shut. Up.*

Luc turns on Mario Bauzá, the trill of the trombone breaking through the quick beat of the percussion, making sense of the chaos. Luc lowers the volume; I see the thirteen little green bars and lean my head against the car seat, letting the music fill up the spaces between the webs.

We drop Tanya off first, then Amy. "Be right back." Luc winks, walking her to the door. He comes back with chapped make-out lips, smelling like perfume. After readjusting, he slides into the Dart and winds his way up the street to my house. We don't talk. Luc lets the car idle in front of the house, our breath and the heater fogging the windows.

"*Guevón*," he finally says. "We're cool, okay? You just need to fucking normal out."

I nod, tapping my fingers on his dashboard, needing a release. "Yeah. I think I'm freaked out about the game and stuff, you know—"

He laughs. "Ah, shit. Not too normal. Then you'd be like all the other white boys at the school. But fuck, man, you're sometimes way out there."

I laugh. I just need to get inside. Talk to Kasey. Everything will be fine.

"See you tomorrow morning," he says.

"Okay. Tomorrow. See ya." I stand outside of the house and watch as Luc turns around the cul-de-sac and drives away, his taillights fading in the distance. My damp shirt sticks to my sweaty back and the wind bites with splinter-sharp teeth. I stop for a second and lean over to squeeze my head between my knees, hoping the intense pain will go away; trying to sweep away the spiders and their webs, using the numbers to rein them in.

They're not supposed to be here anymore.

But they're back.

THREE THE SCRIPT

Wednesday, 7:41 p.m.

Seven forty-one. Seven plus four is eleven plus one is twelve divided by four is three. OK.

Light spills from the kitchen window onto our front lawn. I rub the flamingo's beak and work my way up the front porch. The door's unlocked. Mom's washing dishes. Kasey's watching TV and jumps up when I walk in the door.

"Jacob?" Dad says, coming in from the garage on cue, coveralls coated with a film of sawdust. It's like he has some freak sonic hearing. "Why didn't you answer the phone?"

I look down at my phone. Eight missed calls.

I swallow. "Dad, I swear, I didn't even see the calls until

now." I deliberately turn away from the grandfather clock and try to focus, but I can *hear* it. I can hear the tick and the motion of the pendulum, back and forth, back and forth.

Just focus.

I know, though, if I can work out the numbers, the numbing pain will go away and I'll be able to hear what Dad has to say. The world will become clear again. So I turn, slightly, and glance at the time.

7:43

Seven forty-three. Seven plus four is eleven minus three is eight plus seven is fifteen minus three is twelve divided by three is four. *Fuck. Fuck. Fuck.*

7:44

Seven forty-four. Seven minus four is three plus four is seven. OK.

Kasey nudges me and pushes me to face Dad, the clock just out of sight. Mom comes out of the kitchen and leans against the doorframe. Kasey sits in the chair in front of me, like that will shield me from one of Dad's sermons.

I can hear myself saying, "I'm sorry. I went out with Luc and the guys after practice. To In-N-Out. It's the team tradition since we won a few years ago. I just forgot it was today, forgot to call."

"With what money?" Dad asks.

"I had a few bucks. And I borrowed a little to cover Tanya's dinner too." *And Luc's. And Amy's. Christ.*

"From whom?"

"We're just short five or six bucks." I can tell from the way his eyes have that glazed-over look he's a step from going Jack Torrance on me.

"And how much do you have left?"

I pull out the bills. "Like thirty-five?"

"I can give you some money, Jake," Kasey offers.

"Kasey, stay out of this." Dad says.

Kasey shrinks in her chair and crosses her arms in front of her.

"It's just a few dollars. And it's not like I can be the only guy that doesn't invite a chick out—" I pause and rub my temples, trying to push the gray away just so I can get through this conversation. "I'll take care of it, okay? After soccer season, I'll get a job."

"They waited. They were expecting you to pick the order up."

"I'll pick it up tomorrow. After school."

"When I'm doing double shifts, I expect you to pull your weight here. I don't feel like I'm asking too much of you, Jacob. One errand to pick up the meat so we don't have to eat tuna fish every night." Dad's doing that clench-jaw thing that makes him look like he stepped right out of a Testosterone Nation infomercial.

Tick-tock, tick-tock.

"I'll get it tomorrow. After practice."

"Mr. Hartman said they're expecting a shipment in the

morning. Somebody will be there by six thirty."

I stare at the crisp bills in my hand, creased perfectly down the middle. "Do you, um, have—" I inhale and immediately regret it. My clothes, the money, my hair—everything smells like fast-food restaurant grease.

"He'll give us credit until the end of the month."

"After this weekend, after the game, everything will be taken care of." My voice sounds clear, like what I'm saying really matters.

That stops Dad from pawning my soccer gear to pay for our Hartman Family Meat Pack Number Five with a turhamken sampler included.

The game.

Scouts. Scholarships. Future.

That's something he wants more than me. A future. I hate playing that card, but tonight I just need to get to my room. Tomorrow I'll figure out how to make up for it—for being the total asshole son. Tomorrow I won't screw up.

"UCLA, Maryland," the school names slip off my tongue. My thoughts come slowly through the heavy fog. I have to choose my words carefully. And I wonder if anybody's head ever got so full of lies, it just snapped off and rolled away. It's so easy to lie, to pretend everything is okay when the only things that matter to me right now are getting to my room; the numbers; getting down the clocks; clearing up the fucking mess in my mind.

My voice sounds calm.

I know the script. "Saturday everything will work out with the game, winning our third championship. My grades are good enough. . . ."

Mom sighs and squeezes Dad's shoulder. Her hands are chapped, fingernails gnawed to nothing. Dad reaches up to her for a second, but a shadow crosses his eyes and his hand falls lamely at his side.

Mom doesn't notice and comes to me, wrapping me in her frail arms, saying, "Get some rest. You'll need it. Don't worry about the groceries. I can help take care of it too." Dark shadows circle her bloodshot eyes, and she walks upstairs, pausing at the entryway, staring at the car keys that jangle in her hand. When Mom gets like this, it's like watching a stone pelt glass. At first there's a slight imperfection, but soon the whole thing is covered with cracks until the glass shatters into jewel-size pieces. Since Mom lost her job and can't get another one, Dad's working overtime and a half. So Kase and I are the ones stuck picking up and gluing the pieces back together.

Not this week, Mom. Just keep it together this week, I think, and push back my anger. I turn to Dad, but he looks away, his jaw clenched. He's checked out. "I've got a lot of work to do," Dad says. He rubs his temples, nods, and heads to the garage. We hear the roar of the sander as it comes to life. The high-pitched shrill gives way to a dull hum as it slides across the wood. Tiny dust particles of winter-smelling pine float through the air.

I swallow the ball of *what if*s that has formed in the back of my throat. *What if I hadn't been able to control the spiders tonight at In-N-Out?*

What if I'd said more crazy shit out loud?

I'll call Luc before bed.

No.

That's even crazier—retracing thoughts and conversation. It's like unraveling the knotted webs in my brain.

Impossible.

What if . . .

Thousands of spider legs scratch the inside of my brain like they're burrowing holes into my cranium. Blinding pain.

I wait for the auras and hope to get to my room to get the numbers organized. I can't get a migraine today. Not today. Not this week. I think about the game, the team; the magic; the numbers; the time.

Once I get the numbers worked out, I can see the real world. It's not so confusing anymore. They keep things in order.

Our team wins because of them. Mom, Dad, and Kasey are safe because of them. Maybe Luc and my other friends are safe too. Because of the numbers.

Because I have the magic.

FIVE ABERRATION

Wednesday, 8:05 p.m.

Eight-oh-five. Eight plus five is thirteen. OK.

Kase trails after me with three sandwiches and a glass of milk that teeters on the edge of a tray. When she makes sandwiches, they are perfect towers of order: Everything lines up with the bread; lettuce, cheese, and ham don't flop and dangle over the sides; no mustard goops out when I hold the sandwich in my hands. Then she cuts them in symmetrical triangles, like she knows I need the sides even or something.

Light spills from under Mom and Dad's bedroom door, and the muffled sound of hammering comes from the garage.

I shiver and pull a sweatshirt on. Kase sits next to me, wrapped in my ratty blanket. We sit in silence, leaning against the foot of my bed, while I chew seven times on the left, six on the right, swallow, then switch.

The searing pain in my temples ebbs in the comfort of my room. When I finish eating, I get up to open the curtains, cracking the window just a touch. The crescent moon glows. It's one of those crisp nights when the sky looks like a silver colander with light pouring through its holes.

Kasey's unusually quiet. Quiet is not her modus operandi. I think half her caloric expenditure comes from talking. She usually uses up all her cell minutes within the first week of each month and begs to use my phone because she knows I never use any minutes because I never call anybody.

Ever.

I turn away from the night sky and ask, "Did you do your homework?"

"Yes."

"Okay. Tell me about your day."

It has to be done this way. We do this. Every evening. And if she's not home, I call her.

She pauses, then seems to forget about me squandering all of our food money on a burger joint, animatedly telling me about the freshman talent show. But I can tell she's holding back. I close my eyes and lean my head against my bed. My teeth chatter. Goddamn it's cold.

Kase leaves and comes out with some cash. "Here. This should cover it. And keep what's left for this weekend."

"Where'd you get this?" I ask.

She shrugs.

I shake my head and shove the bills back into her hand. "No. This is for you and the theater classes you want to take at the Brewery Arts Center this summer. I'll get a job after soccer. I'll take care of it."

"Then pay me back," she says.

"No." Because I know I won't. I never get around to paying anybody back, which does not bode well for a degree in business or economics—the two top careers that came up when we had our career-day meetings with Counselor Lafer and some other college counselors. My third choice, though, turned out to be water-treatment worker.

Go figure.

Kasey peels off half the bills and gives them to me. "You'll pay me back. This time you will." I so appreciate Kasey's eternal faith that I'll change into somebody worth something. But it only reminds me of the fact that it's my job to make the world right for her—easier—not the other way around.

"Thanks, though, K," I say. "I owe you one."

"Um, no. You owe me fifty."

"Yeah, Miss Literal. Got it."

"*And* a favor."

"What kind of favor?"

"It shouldn't matter."

"Well, it does. Like are we talking digging-shallow-graves-in-the-backyard kind of favor or cover-for-you-when-you-want-to-go-hang-out-with-friends kind of favor?"

"Can't you just say you owe me one?"

"I owe you one." I close my eyes again, welcoming the silence.

"You know how much work this takes?"

"Huh?" I open my eyes.

"Maintenance, Jake. High maintenance to keep the edge—to keep with the right crowd."

"Aren't you the leader of the right crowd?" I ask. Kasey always has a following.

"Today. But it doesn't come for free. My popularity is inherited, you know."

"Inherited?"

"Look at me."

I look.

"Look real hard."

"Yeah. So?"

"Let's be real. Mousy brown hair—a bit frizzy. Skinny. No talent."

"Kase—"

"Aunt Marian." Kasey does a Vanna White hand

flourish, head to toe, then slumps back against the bed.

"Aunt Marian?" Aunt Marian is Mom's sister who wears wooden clogs and pilly sweaters that smell like a weird mix of mall animal store, Vicks VapoRub, mothballs, and vinegar. She wears her frizzy hair tied back in a loose ponytail and raises ostriches in central Nevada. "Now that you mention it—"

"Ohmygod!" The tears well up in Kasey's eyes. I forget that Kasey's prepubescence is gone, hidden under this power-hungry popularity shell.

"Just kidding, K. C'mon." I try to get her to settle down. "It was a really bad joke."

She chokes out the words, "Never. Been. Kissed."

I squirm. "Well, I sure as hell don't want to hear about it if you have."

"That's not the point. Everything about me is average. Except for you." She wipes her hand across her nose.

I hand her a Kleenex and try to focus on her, not the line of glistening snot in her arm hair.

Kase throws back her shoulders and says, "Maintenance, Jake. If I want to stay at the top, I've got to start *doing* things to show I deserve to be at the top. You leave this year, and then I'll be left to swim the social waters on my own. I'm just saying it's all about keeping it together, being with the right people at the right time."

"Wouldn't it just be a lot easier to have friends you like?"

"*Nobody* has friends she likes in high school. *C'mon.*"

And I think about it, about my friends. Friend. Luc. Sometimes I don't know if we're friends because we're friends or because we've known each other so long now, we have to be. Because there's too much shit there—too much history. We'd probably get our asses kicked if anybody knew that Luc and I used to swipe his mom's tights to play superheroes. I was always the Green Lantern and Luc was Aquaman. You see, nobody calls the real superheroes flaming when they wear tights. But the day Luc's dad found us playing, I seriously thought that thick vein on his forehead was going to explode and spurt blood all over us major manga style.

Maybe because the blue ones Luc wore had some lacy shit on them. I dunno.

"Anyway . . ." Kase keeps talking about how she needs to carve her niche in the social hierarchy of Carson City before I leave; how once I'm gone, she's the only one left to keep this family looking half normal. "It's like you have an aura about you—this cool, mysterious thing that attracts people to you. You get away with being weird. And next year you're leaving. And I'll be here. Stuck. With *them*." She hisses *them* like we're being raised by inbred Appalachian hillbillies. "It's gonna be a nightmare without you. What if Mom has a freakout?" Kasey pauses. "Let me rephrase that. How long before Mom has another total freakout? And Dad just—"

"Does nothing?" Our family lives by Dad's philosophy:

If you can't see blood, it doesn't hurt. So how can you fix a make-believe problem?

"Exactly," Kasey says.

My head really hurts, and all I want to do is get organized—bring order back to the day. "I'm not weird," I say.

"Jake, weird can be good, too. Your kind of weird. All I'm saying is that being your sister won't cut it anymore. I need to act. Move forward. Maintenance. Remember that. You owe me one."

"From the sound of it, you owe me."

Kase scowls.

"Okay, okay. I'll deliver. I promise. All good?"

"All good," she says. "Night, Jake."

I walk her to the hallway and watch as she eases her door shut. The soft sound of sweeping comes from the garage. Mom's room is dark. I stand alone in the hallway, cloaked in gray; the only slit of light that slips through is the tear in the blackout blind covering the upstairs hallway window. It disperses unevenly, tentacles of light disappearing into the shadows, yellow turned to gray, blurring the lines, until everything's distorted like an optical aberration.

It's like we're all suffocating in blackness.

There's something not right about not being able to see the night sky, dawn, the light of the moon and stars and sun.

I retreat to my bedroom and exhale. The only room that's soaked in starlight—the only room that makes sense.

I open the closet feeling a rush of relief as I look up at the clocks on the top shelf. Forty-three, including a ten-hour clock Kasey found for me at an antique sale. I reach up to pull one down, then hesitate.

Not this week. I don't need them.

My neck tenses, and I bite down to hold back the wave of pain.

Not this week.

I run my fingers over the boxes and shut the door, turning to the clock on my nightstand, taking off my watch. I focus on the glowing numbers of the clock.

9:37

Nine thirty-seven. Nine plus three is twelve plus seven is nineteen. OK.

I stare at the time, watching the second hand on my clock with the Indiglo light, then turn away just as it's about to be 9:38. The spiders retreat to wherever they came from. I can feel the webs dissolving in my brain.

I sleep.

SEVEN SANCTUARIES

Thursday, 5:06 a.m.

I open my left eye, count to three, and watch as the blurry numbers take form. Then I open my right eye. Too early. It's still middle-of-the-night black outside. Coach shouldn't have called this early-morning practice.

This isn't right. It won't work.

It breaks the routine.

It messes everything up.

My cell phone beeps. Luc.

DntBL8

I squeeze my eyes closed but feel the glowing numbers from the clock through my thin lids.

It's no big deal.

But it's dark. No light of dawn.

It doesn't matter.

Everything matters.

My phone beeps again. Luc's on a message frenzy this morning. I open my eyes and stare at the glowing numbers on the clock.

5:08

Five-oh-eight. Five plus eight equals thirteen. OK. Eight minus five equals three. OK. Three plus three equals six plus eight equals fourteen plus three equals seventeen. OK. Seventeen plus eight equals twenty-five minus five equals twenty plus eight equals twenty-eight. Fuck. Minus five equals twenty-three. OK.

Five-oh-eight and fifty-five—

I slip my left foot out from under the covers and count. *One, two, three.*

Fifty-six, fifty-seven—

Right foot. *One, two, three.*

Fifty-eight, fifty-nine.

It'll be okay.

Up.

5:09

It's black outside except for the soft glow of the corner streetlight. The light sputters for a second, and I hold my breath until the blinking stops, counting the seconds for it to steady.

That's new.

The light from the streetlamp hasn't had problems before.

It bothers me.

I stare at it while holding my breath. Thirty-seven seconds. It's cheating, holding out longer on thirty-seven, but I'll make up for it.

My eyes are heavy and I rub them to wake up. I can't mess around this morning, can't be late.

Frost frames the window in perfect symmetry.

I pull on the blue sweats with parallel stripes down the sides. Then my left sock, right sock, left shoe, right shoe. My shirt slips over my arms at the same time, perched on top of my head. I tug the shirt over my face, the soft fabric easing down and settling on my shoulders.

The glowing numbers on the clock change to 5:10, then 5:11. Magic. Digital clocks—no ticks but they still know when to pass from one minute to the next. They were invented in 1956. Good number. Good year. *One plus nine is ten minus five is five plus six is eleven. OK.* Good year.

I take one PowerBar Gel with a few sips of water. Vanilla. *Ack.* Dad got a pack at Costco, and I've been ingesting vanilla-flavored gel for the past month and a half.
5:13

Fuck.

I missed when the time changed. Totally zoned out. I don't know how many seconds have passed. I'll wait. I watch as it changes from 5:13 to 5:14 and rush downstairs, skipping steps eight and four—creaky. Unlucky. Then I tap the grandfather clock three times with each hand and use both hands to open the front door, stepping out into the morning.

Jesus. It's the freaking arctic. I look at the thermometer but can't see through the frosted glass. When I inhale, it feels like a film of ice enters and covers my lungs, moving on to freeze every organ in my body.

I can see the streetlight start to sputter again, so I turn away from it, pretending I don't notice the erratic blinking. *Fuck.* I stop for a second and consider waiting, holding my breath, counting the seconds, but I look at my wristwatch. Five seventeen already.

I can't be late.

Coach will kill me.

5:17

Good number, though. *Five minus one is four plus seven is eleven.* I'm tempted to wait until 5:23. 5:23. Three primes that make one big prime. Absolutely perfect. I pause. But I don't have time and I'd be way late. Luc is cool about shit, but I don't think anybody, no matter how cool he is, would get that I have to hold out for primes. Hard to explain that kind of stuff, even to the guy who used to tie string to his mom's wooden fork, pretending it was Aquaman's harpoon left hand, while wearing colorful tights.

Maybe he *would* get it.

Nah. That was kid stuff, the stuff that's easy to blow off. This is *different*. It's weird that the people we spend the most time with know the least about us. Maybe Luc has some fucked-up shit he hides.

Nah. Too weird.

It's okay. Another time. I force my feet to move down the steps, keeping my back to the streetlight.

One, two, three.

One, two, three.

My shoes slap against the damp concrete as I jog to practice, the pungent smell of damp sagebrush tickling my nose. The parking lot is dotted with cars, a clump of them at the gate of the field. I fall into step behind the guys while we work our way to the track.

When we get to the field, the blades of grass are frosty damp—like miniature ice sculptures that crunch underfoot. I pull off my running shoes and put on my cleats. Then we begin conditioning, breaking the glassy silence with pounding feet and heavy breathing—all moving together in a Gregorian chant–like trance.

We're all on the same time, a synchronized *tick-tock*, *tick-tock*. We watch Coach and follow his signals, keeping an easy pace. Too much is riding on Saturday for any of us to get hurt.

We begin drills. The ball soars across the field in a

blur. Its grooved surface molds to my cleats, and the field opens up before me, everything else murky and gray. Crisp, focused, I become the creator on the field—finding the hole, the open man. Everything comes together; no webs; no spiders; no numbers; just me and the ball. The ball curves past Diaz into the goal. We begin another half-field scrimmage. I scoop it over Kalleres; Grundy back-passes to Keller, who drills it, Diaz skidding across the wet grass, grasping it in his gloved hands.

We play. I score. We win.

Because of the magic.

"Jesus, man," Diaz says after our last drill, "I swear we all just get in your way out there. Fuck, what you got in those shoes, *gabacho locochón*?" He wipes sweat from his brow; white puffs of breath come out and dissolve in the cold morning air.

I laugh and take off my cleats, the grass now wet from melted frost—no more crystal palaces. The guys grab their stuff and head back to their cars.

It's a perfect morning.

"*Guevón*, you gonna run home or do you want a ride?" Luc says, and heads to his car.

"A ride." I follow Luc out to the lot and open the passenger door of his cathedral—the 1972 Dodge Dart—and respectfully click it shut. Even though Luc's stuck going to mass every weekend with his family, this is his religion.

Unfortunately, he expects all of us to pay our tithes and passes around this old hat for gas money every time he fills up. It sucks because he has to fill up the guzzler like ten times more than guys with more fuel-efficient vehicles.

But showing up in the Dart is worth it. Luc's worth it.

Mornings like this are worth it, sanctuaries in the chaos.

Luc slides into the driver's seat and cranks *Locos por Juana* up. I bump the volume up one more to seventeen notches. He nods approvingly. We leave the parking lot, the gravel crunching under the Dart's tires.

I lean my head back and close my eyes, listening to the rhythmic beat, sorry the ride has to end, because I'm in that spot between awake and asleep when everything feels dreamlike and safe.

ELEVEN TIME TRIAL

Thursday, 6:19 a.m.

Six nineteen. Nine minus one is eight minus six is two. OK.

It's that in-between time before the sun has risen but after the curtain of night has been lifted. The streetlight is off. I walk in the front door, tapping the pink flamingo's beak on the way in, the tip faded from years of taps. It's a tacky prize Mom got at some raffle a long time ago. Dad hates it. Mom says she's not going to give away the only thing she's ever won. Kasey's pretty indifferent. "Giant pink birds really aren't my thing. But I'm not going to go all antiwaterfowl on you either." And I need to rub the fucking beak or my hands get all itchy.

The flamingo stays.

The house smells like burned coffee. Mom bangs around the kitchen, faded flower wallpaper and mud-yellow linoleum giving the kitchen that overcast-day look. Dad comes downstairs, goes into the kitchen, and dumps the brown sludge, rinsing out the caramel residue from the pot.

"I like it strong," she apologizes. And it bugs the shit out of me that Mom has to apologize for the way she likes to drink her own coffee. Let her spoon it out if she wants. It's her coffee.

The pot percolates and bubbles, but the new brew doesn't cover up the burn smell.

I look at the grandfather clock.

6:22

Six twenty-two. Six plus two is eight plus two is ten divided by two is five. OK.

It works.

But something about it bugs me, so I stare at the clock, counting the seconds to 6:23.

"You're going to be late, Jacob. Mr. Hartman is expecting you at half past six. You better hurry if you expect to get there and back here before school starts."

"Late," I mutter, the numbers blurring. 6:23. God-damnit. 6:23.

"What do you want for breakfast?" Mom peeks around the kitchen corner, her cheeks sunken and pale, a stark contrast to the raccoon-black circles. The car keys are on the table beside a crinkled map of Carson City with red X marks all over it. Christ. She probably drove all over Carson, retracing her steps from yesterday all night long again. She does that—looking for accidents she might've caused, unreported hits and runs, retracing her steps to stores, carrying receipts to prove she hasn't stolen anything.

In a state that's open twenty-four hours, retracing steps is hell. Sometimes I think we should move to Utah. Everything there probably closes at five thirty or something.

Dad brushes past me and sits at the table, opening up the paper to the business section. His eyes are puffy and bloodshot too. He mutters about bailouts, IRAs, oil prices, and wars. He takes it all personally, like the economy went to shit just to piss him off.

"Jacob," he says through the paper. "Get moving. One more school tardy and you get in-house suspension. And that means no soccer. No Saturday game. No scouts. No future." And that last word—*future*—lingers in the air. He tosses me the "last warning" notice the school sent out to my parents. "Jacob . . ."

I look at the dates with big red marks on them. Principal Vaughn has signed the bottom of the notice in tiny, squiggly letters. Fucking tight ass. "I've been late seven times?"

Dad sets the newspaper on the table and nods. He does it kind of like Godzilla—like somebody's shoved a steel rod in his spine, making his neck unmovable. "Mr. Hartman is waiting." The game begins. Dad sets a nearly impossible goal, and I run my ass off trying to make it. Today it's called the Hartman Meats Time Trial, in which all opponents must get the family meat pack, turhamken included, put them in the deep freeze, and arrive at school on time. *Your future depends on it.*

Seven tardies. *Seven. OK.*

"Don't mess this up." Dad's talking through the paper again. *This* means future. Mine or his, though, I'm not sure. "Mr. Hartman is waiting for you."

I stare at the clock, the minute hand slipping into place. 6:25

Six twenty-five. Six plus two is eight plus five is thirteen. OK.

Mom looks from above the refrigerator door, her eyes pleading with me.

I sometimes feel like this entire house is a wind-up toy just one turn away from exploding wires, levers, and coils all over the place.

"Yeah," I say. "I'll get there." I walk upstairs, skipping steps four and eight, and move toward the shower. I hesitate. I don't have time.

But I've got to have a shower.

My palms sweat and I stand in front of the bathroom door, holding my breath, counting to seventeen, then starting over again. I do this three times.

Fuck it.

I don't need to shower.

Who gives a shit?

But I need to shower.

Fuck.

It's A schedule. I can be late—just a little bit.

No big deal.

Kasey stomps past me in the hallway, pinching her nose. "You know, in this country we shower every day and use a thing called *deodorant*." She glares. She has to leave the house a good half hour earlier than I do. But it's not like I can *make* Luc take her to school. Who knows who he's gonna pick up? He's King Carpool. Especially when he's low on gas.

"Kase, I took the bus when I was a freshman too."

One foot in the bathroom, one foot out. I almost burst out laughing because I am the hokey pokey incarnate. Fuck, I'm such a joke.

She huffs. "Dad went Cracked Pepper and Olive Oil this morning when he saw the tardy notice. Lucky he didn't see it last night, because that with the In-N-Out incident would've sent him totally Thin Crisps Quattro Formaggio."

We have a code for Dad going nuts—"crackers." Saltines means he's pretty sane. But when Kasey goes all out, trying to find the weirdest flavor on the shelves, I know Dad's pretty flipped. "Yeah. I've gotta get going. Can't be late. My *future* depends on it." I smirk.

"Butthead."

"Number three," I say.

"Yeah, yeah. Enchanted number three. Whoopee. This Saturday, yet again, I get to be crushed under the giant shadow of Magic Martin, M&M, while in his greatest, final act, he wins the championship, a full-ride scholarship paving his way to world fame and glory while leaving me to rot in what-nobody-knows-is-the-capital-of-Nevada."

"I'll get Luc to take you to school the rest of the week."

"You will?" Kasey raises her eyebrows.

"I'll try."

She scowls.

"That's all I've got."

"Yeah. Yeah." She looks at her watch. "Better hurry." She skips downstairs. For being a popularity-hungry freshman, Kase is borderline cool.

I take the quickest shower in history and end up with a film of soap on my left shin. I get dressed and run back into the bathroom to rinse off the soap. It just takes a second. Then I'm out and running down the stairs, grabbing Mom's car keys from the entryway. "Be right back," I say, rushing out the door, careful to tap the grandfather clock and open the door with both hands on the knob. I turn away from the flamingo. That's only for going inside.

6:43

Six forty-three. Six plus four is ten plus three is thirteen. OK.

42

It's like everything is coming together so easy this morning.

"Your breakfast!" Mom runs outside balancing a scrambled-egg burrito and cup of coffee, three tablespoons of cream, three sugars, in her hands. I touch her cheek—her skin dry, paper-thin. She looks older than she should.

At least when she was working at the Do-It-Yourself Craft Emporium, she had something to do. At one point, everything in our house smelled like cinnamon sticks and hot glue. But Mom got canned a few weeks ago. She's been unraveling ever since. "They'll probably hire for Christmas season."

"Probably," she says, shoving the food at me.

I take a big bite of the breakfast burrito. "Really."

"Don't talk with your mouth full. Drive carefully. Watch the school zones."

I swallow. "Sorry." It's nice when Mom's a mom.

6:45

Six forty-five. Six plus four is ten plus five is fifteen minus four is eleven. OK.

Good enough.

I peel out of the driveway and head to Hartman Meats.

THIRTEEN MEMORIES UNEARTHED

Thursday, 6:53 a.m.

Six fifty-three. Six plus five is eleven minus three is eight minus five is three. OK.

Mera Hartman is standing behind the counter looking like one of those hazmat guys who have to be covered head to toe so some freak bacteria won't make them bleed out of their eyeballs.

"You're late!" she hollers at me through a paper mask, her eyes covered in plastic goggles. "They told me you'd be here at six thirty. It's six"—she points to her watch with a thick-mitted hand—"six fifty-three. So I'm stuck on a Thursday morning in the slaughterhouse waiting for the least reliable human being on the planet. Thank you very much." She makes a funny shuffling sound when she moves because of the layers of heavy-duty plastic aprons she's piled on.

I kind of think Mera takes complying with food-sanitary conditions a little far.

"Hey," I say lamely, and glance at my watch.

6:54

Six fifty-four. Six times five is thirty plus four is thirty-four minus five is twenty-nine. OK.

"Here." She shoves the Family Meat Pack Number Five at me over the counter.

"Thanks," I say. "Sorry for making you wait."

Her goggles are fogged up, so I don't know if she even notices me half waving when I leave. I haul the meat out to Mom's car, passing some old guy who looks like he's in a big hurry rushing into the shop.

I slump into the front seat and exhale, glad it's over so I can go home and get on with the day.

Any encounter with Mera is weird. We all used to be friends. She was always Black Orchid or Boodikka, depending on Mrs. Camacho's tights supply.

Then I just stopped calling.

And so did she.

So it was like we broke up. I remember the day we did: the day after Mera's brothers had spray-painted CANNED

LABOR FOUND HERE on the side of Luc's house, littering the yard with empty Spic and Span spray bottles.

Luc, Mera, and I spent that whole morning scrubbing off the ugly words until they faded into nothing. We had to get them washed off before Luc's dad came home. I had seen Luc's bruises when we were little. Mera and I had. We just pretended not to.

When we finished, Mera left and returned with a paper plate of salami and cheese, the salami grease seeping through the flimsy plate. She looked from me to Luc.

"Another day, Mera," Luc said, tossing the last of the Spic and Span bottles into the plastic recycling bin.

But that other day never came.

Mera looks at me through the shop window, and my stomach sinks. Familiar barbs of pain work their way up the base of my neck. Maybe because of the sputtering light.

Just as I shift the car into gear, Mera comes running out to me, flapping her arms.

Fuck. The money. I roll down the window and hand her what I've got, keeping Kasey's loan for me. It's total shit having to explain to somebody your family can't afford meat. Maybe we should just stick to eating tuna fish, mercury poisoning and all. Then we could win a sweet lawsuit about how Tasty Tuna made us grow extra ears or something. I look over at the discount food mart. I don't think they extend credit for their generic-brand sodas and cans of tuna, though. "I thought my dad talked to your dad. About paying"—I clear my throat—"about paying the rest at the end of the month."

Mera pulls up her mask. "Whatever. I don't give a rat's ass about when you pay for the murder of these animals. But I need your help. That man needs *sausages*."

I shrug. "So?"

"So? *Sausages*." She says it the way everybody in my family talked about my grandma having *cancer*—in that whispered, conspiratorial tone. *Cancer*. Mera's heavy-mitted hand grasps my elbow. "The *sausages* are in the walk-in. In the back." She shudders. "With all the other animal corpses. Help. Me."

I realize that the longer I wait for a logical explanation from a girl who grew up stuffing sausages in her garage, the longer it'll take to leave, and I'll never get anywhere on time. So I roll up the window and turn off the car, following Mera back into her dad's shop.

The man half smiles, half waves, and taps his foot impatiently. Mera says under her breath, "They're in the back—in the boxes. Can you just get me some?"

"Some? How much is some?"

"Just take a box out, okay?" Mera smiles at the customer and turns to me. "I *can't* go in there again today."

I nod and head toward the walk-in freezer, trying to ignore the tingling at the back of my neck. There's nothing wrong. I'll just get a box of sausages.

A cold current of air circulates, recycling that butcher-shop smell of Clorox and raw cuts of dead animal flesh. I stare at the worn floor with rust-colored stains all over it, counting the square tiles in the hallway.

Mera hollers. "Did you find them?"

"Just a sec." I pull my eyes from the tile and open the walk-in freezer door.

I hear the rustle of her plastic suit, and Mera brushes by me. "Just hold the door, then," she says working her way to the back of the walk-in. She mumbles, ducking under massive ribs and flanks of meat hanging on hooks. Legs, gray-colored hooves, and red-colored animal parts dangle from the ceiling. I step into the freezer, one foot in, one foot out. It's like I'm always straddling, one foot in the place I'm supposed to be and the other in the place I want to be.

Stuck.

I try to ignore the tight feeling I'm getting in my chest, steadying my breathing. "You okay in here?" I step all the way in. "Christ," I mutter. "Hello, Donner party."

"Ha. Ha." Her voice is muffled by some boxes. "Help me out, okay? And don't," she says when she stands up, watching the door click closed behind me, "shut. The. Door."

I turn around and see the handle is broken—dangling from its hinge. I push on the door, but it doesn't budge.

Oh God. No.

"What the . . . What butcher in the world has a broken freezer door? Like isn't this against some kind of regulation or something?" The tingling moves up my spine, thousands of miniature spiders trying to invade my brain again, covering it with thick, sticky webs, until all I feel is sharp pounding and my vision is reduced to black splotches. "Oh Jesus," I say.

Mera jiggles the handle. "Relax. I saw it was broken this morning, hence asking you to hold the door open for me. Ryan was supposed to call for maintenance. . . ."

Everything goes out of focus, gray, except for the raw red splotches of color that hang above us. I push Mera aside and throw myself against the door, my shoulder cracking against the heavy steel. The freezer's walls move in until they're crushing me between them; crushing my chest, snapping rib by rib until my lungs collapse under the pressure, and I gasp for the last bubble of air.

I slump to the floor and stare at the frozen flesh hanging from the ceiling, trying to preserve our dwindling air supply, breathing in bits of refrigerated death. Mera flits around dressed as an Imperial Stormtrooper. She talks about getting her DNA tested because there's no possible way she can share the same genetic makeup as her brother, Ryan . . . blahblahblahblah. Flitflitflit . . . like a fucking hummingbird.

Shut up shut up shutupshutupshutup. Stop. Using. The. Air.

Shutupshutupshutupshutup.

Her words are swallowed by screams.

I inhale and try to focus on the time, the numbers, but can't read the time. My watch face has fogged up. I rub my eyes.

Shutup. Just. Shut. Up.

I can't concentrate on the numbers over the noise—everything that's said bounces back from wall to wall, never fading in the distance because there's nowhere for it to go—Ping-Pong words. Back and forth. Back and forth.

Who's screaming?

> *I gag on the closet's musty death smell. Kasey's shrieks reach me through the jammed-shut door. "I'm coming!" My voice is hoarse, so I kick on the door, again and again—a flurry of kicks until the soles of my feet are raw.*

The door swings open and I stumble into the hallway, lying down, gulping in the stale butcher-shop air. The man and Mera loom over me and stare.

Inhale.

Exhale.

Mera holds a string of kielbasy in her mitted hand. She shoves the goggles up on her head and crouches down, a deep crease between her eyes. "Jake?" she says. The man rubs his nose with a dirty hanky. From my angle I can see his nose is raw and chafed. He peers down at me through thick bifocals. He squints and removes his glasses, wipes them with the crusty corner of his hanky, then replaces them on his bulbous, red nose.

"Well," I say, clearing my throat. "Glad I could be of some service to you, Mera." I sit up slowly, averting my eyes. As soon as I feel the sticky silk web contract, pulling away from the folds in my brain, I stand and brush off my jeans, shoving my trembling hands in my pockets. "If that's all, then?" I say.

What did I do? What did I say?

"I think you'd better lay off those Starbucks espressos, kid. You know, when I was your age, we didn't drink a half gallon of coffee in the morning like you kids do nowadays. That's gotta be bad for your nervous system. Think of the garbage you're putting in your engine, son." He says this while grabbing the ten-foot strand of pale intestine-encased spiced meat.

I nod and half salute him, trying to deflect Mera's gaze, wishing she'd just put her goggles back on. When I get into the parking lot, my lungs fill with the fresh November air. I lean my head against the car door, welcoming the cold metal on my burning cheeks. I heave my breakfast burrito; it drips down the side of the car into an acidic puddle on the asphalt. My mouth has the slight aftertaste of vanilla gel. The only thing I have to wipe up the door of the car is a flyer for the Haunted Stairway Society. I crumple that up and try to wipe off the side of Mom's car and end up spreading the egg chunks.

Mera and the man stare at me from inside the store. My chest shudders. I haven't thought about that night for a long time and hate that my mind woke up the dead memory.

Memories should be like dead relatives—buried.

Just get it together. Nothing happened.

But I don't know what I did. Or said.

It's just Mera.

7:21

The numbers on my watch pop out at me, and I massage the face, watching the second hand tick around 360 degrees until time begins again.

7:22

Tick-tock, tick-tock.

Seven twenty-two. Seven plus two is nine plus two is eleven. OK.

SEVENTEEN KEEPING ORDER

Thursday, 7:31 a.m.

Seven thirty-one. Seven plus three is ten plus one is eleven. OK.

When I pull into the driveway, Luc is standing outside, talking to Mom, holding a school lunch the size of a grocery sack.

Mom's there, picking on her hangnails, eyes darting between Luc, the sandwiches, and the house. She looks relieved when I drive up.

"Mom, we'll *never* get to class on time if you don't put the meat away. Can you? Please?" I'm out of breath and feel a dull pressure behind my eyeballs. I wonder if they're bulging.

"Of course, honey," she says.

"Really, Mom. You've got to put the meat away. Like now."

"I will." She pushes her hair behind her ears and strains to smile.

The pink flamingo's beak peeks from behind Mom. And I want to touch it, just rub it. But I can't because then I'd have to go in and start over.

Start over.

That might make everything better.

I shouldn't have left before dawn. It's not how things go. Always wait for the sun, but with early practice, I had no choice. I shove my hands into my pants pockets, balling my fists so I can't get them out of the jeans.

There's no time.

Just one day, it'll be okay. Just once.

"Nice talking to you, Mrs. Martin," Luc says, bowing out and heading to the car.

"Luc's got your lunch, honey," she says. "I didn't know what you'd want—ham, tuna, turkey—so I made all three. Did you eat your breakfast?"

"Sure, Mom. It was great." Both times.

Luc and I jump into the car. He drums his fingers on the dashboard to 3 Pesos—his get-pumped-for-a-game music. Before we pull out, he cranks up the volume and says, "Your mom tripping again?" He waves the sack bulging with sandwiches at me—one of those telltale signs that Mom's spiraling into the black zone. Dad gets pissed, saying he spends half his paycheck feeding the team when Mom's having a spell.

"Yeah. She's sick." That's what Dad calls it when Mom gets freaked about things: sick, like she's got the flu. It's gotta be hard for him to keep a lid on the House of the Weird. But everybody seems to like to play along.

Mera and I did with Luc's bruises. Don't ask. Don't tell.

He pulls out the ham and cheese and rips into it. "Nice." He swallows and grabs my coffee to wash it down. Crumbs of bread float in the rim of the lid.

He hands it back to me and I shake my head. "It's all yours."

"What took you so long at the meat house?"

"You don't want to know," I say, and look at my watch.
7:32

Seven thirty-two. Seven plus three is ten plus two is twelve minus seven is five. OK.

Luc puts the car into gear and pulls away from the house. I can see Mom's silhouette in the kitchen window.

Luc's talking about something—something about the game on Saturday. But I feel like I'm floating away from his words, his voice, so I hold my breath and count to forty-seven, then twenty-three. His voice gets louder, clearer.

I look back down at my watch.

7:33

Seven thirty-three. Three primes. Seven plus three is ten plus three is thirteen. OK.

Great number.

I twist my watch around my wrist so I can't see the face, just wanting to keep everything at 7:33 for the rest of the day.

Focus.

And it's like going back to the time and numbers have screwed me up. I was okay for the last few weeks, then something got all fucked up. I retrace my steps from this morning and last night, trying to figure out when I messed up the routine, when the dead memory slipped in.

It's like finding a glitch in a computer program, then reprogramming it. That's how my brain works; that's what keeps the order.

Seven thirty-three.

I unclasp my watch and shove it into my backpack, ignoring the chill that climbs up my spine. I need to focus on the game—go timeless the next couple of days until I can get it under control. I just need my mind to jell and stop racing so much—too much rides on these next few days.

My future.

So I don't need the time. The numbers.

And for just a moment my mind believes what I tell it. Everything that happened this morning becomes a hazy memory, dulled by the thump of 3 Pesos. The tingling stops. The spiders sleep. I turn the volume up to seventeen so the music crowds the rest of my thoughts out. We rock our way into the school parking lot.

look down at my wrist. No watch.

Luc smiles, "Plenty of time, man. Seven forty-five."

Seven forty-five. Seven plus four is eleven minus five is six plus seven is thirteen. OK.

We make it way before the first bell rings, walking through the side door, waiting for three people to go in ahead of us. Then I slip in the door without touching anything. I haven't touched the handle of a school entrance or exit since I was a freshman.

I think about how weird that is and that nobody's ever noticed.

Luc pauses in the doorway. We stand in that place

between the outside door and inside door. I can tell Luc is trying to figure out how to make his entrance. He always makes an entrance, no matter where we go.

"Time to shine," he says.

I have been holding my breath for thirteen seconds when he finally speaks. Thirteen. Good number.

"C'mon." We work our way to the indoor courtyard where half the school is gathered talking about Saturday's game. Banners hang from rafters. Before I can get away, we're shoved into a blizzard of blue and white streamers, confetti, and spray string. The cheerleaders and our other teammates surround us, and the Senator mascot does some weird break-dance routine. They circle us; we're closed in with nowhere to go. I clutch my lunch sack, back myself against a column, and look for Luc.

Tick-tock.

Luc's too busy doing some Colombian grind with Amy to find my escape route. I'm on my own.

Fuck. Inhale. *Thirty-nine, forty, forty-one.* Exhale. Then I begin again, counting the seconds, wiping the perspiration from my forehead, searching for a clock until I find one hanging just thirty feet in front of us.

It's like watching a reel of my last two days backward, searching through the times, trying to figure out what went wrong.

The fucking streetlight.

I shouldn't have cheated and held my breath longer on thirty-seven. I should've just started counting again. The right way. Then I wouldn't be here. And I can think of another million things I could've done to change this—make this not happen.

I inhale again, but this time air doesn't enter my lungs. All I breathe in is perfume, body odor, hair spray, and the canned smell of spray string. I gasp for breath and lean my head back against the column, looking up into the open space of the courtyard. *Keep cool*, I think. And it's like I can hear myself talk—which isn't myself—saying, "Right on. Yeah. We're gonna rock it on Saturday." But it feels like my airways have been totally cut off. My diaphragm won't contract. I'm about seventeen seconds away from shoving my face into Mom's paper bag of sandwiches.

I need out.

Now.

And our eyes lock.

Mera.

She stares at me and I worry that her eyes will dry up and fall out of her head if she doesn't blink soon. She *was* Bordewich School's fourth-grade staring champ. But now, in high school, it's just creepy.

Just blink, goddamnit. And I count the seconds until she does—*twenty-three*. Kids at school call her UNICEF 'cause she has that sunken-cheek look you see on those ads for third-world countries.

I close my eyes. *Go away.*

I need the numbers.

But malnourished Mera's head is blocking the fucking clock.

Christ.

I've got to get grounded.

Kasey.

What would she say about Mera?

Inhale.

Crackers.

What would she say about me if she knew who I *really* was?

I brush the thought off and think Baked Whole-Grain Wheat Rosemary and Olive Oil. Kasey helps. She always helps.

Thirty-eight, thirty-nine, forty, forty-one. Exhale.

The bell rings; five minutes to get to class.

Late.

Seven tardies. Now eight.

Tick-tock, tick-tock.

I can feel people moving away and open my eyes. The courtyard empties. The spiders crawl from my brain back to the top of my spine. It's gonna be hell to keep them there. They've come awake twice now.

Mera stares at me like I'm some kind of zoo animal.

I lean on my knees, feeling weak, wiping the sweat from my forehead, pushing my hair back behind my ears. Dad's one allowance—long hair.

Mera's still staring. She's quiet. But a loud, cacophonous kind of silent that rattles in my mind. It's like all those words she never said to me and Luc have settled inside her and seep through her pores.

I'll just not look her way. I've done it since we were twelve, I can do it until I get through the weekend. She reminds me of things. Too many things. I need to sort through the webs.

The second bell rings.

Rushed footsteps echo in the huge courtyard as the last students rush to their classes, disappearing in the adjoining hallways. The smells dissipate and I breathe in the stale school air, tapping the column with both hands before heading to my locker.

I'm late.

Fuck them.

It's A schedule. I can be late. Mr. Adams won't count it. I shake the confetti from my hair, and it drifts to the floor. When I stand up, my head pounds and I feel woozy, so I work my way to the water fountain and gulp down the icy liquid. It dribbles down my chin. I drink, counting to forty-one.

I pull my watch out and slip it back on my wrist. Just for today.

I can be late.

I'm Magic Martin.

I'm the star center midfielder of Carson High School. Our state championship game is this Saturday, November 5, against Bishop Gorman High School.

And we can't lose.

We have the magic.

TWENTY-THREE THE DOUBTING

Thursday, 8:00 a.m.

Eight o'clock. Eight. Shit number. My palms feel clammy.

I knock on the door three times with each hand and peek in.

"Nice of you to show up, Mr. Martin," Mr. Adams says over his glasses. "You now have ten minutes fewer than your classmates to finish the quiz."

Some girls giggle in the back of the class. I catch Tanya's eye and wonder if she's told anybody about yesterday—about the french fries and greasing up the vinyl booth with a gallon of sweat. I half smile, trying to act like everything's normal. I should be used to acting normal by now.

And even though Tanya reminds me of a yappy rat dog, I feel the blood draining from my heart and heading south. She's wearing an extra-extra-small Carson Senators shirt that creeps up when she reaches up to sharpen her pencil. Individually tattooed dandelion fluffs settle on her lower back, leading my eyes to the Never-Never-but-Maybe-If-I'm-a-Lucky-Bastard Land.

Christ. That's all I need. Get a boner in AP history. I wonder which shade of red my face is about now. Red. At least it's a primary color.

Think of something. Stop the flow.

Christ.

Mr. Adams clears his throat and thrusts a paper at me with rough hands and gnawed-on hangnails. "Now you have eleven minutes fewer."

I go limp. Pop quiz'll do it.

I look at the clock.

8:01

Eight-oh-one. Eight minus one is seven. OK. Eight plus one is nine plus eight is seventeen. OK.

I grab the paper and get to my desk, turning away from the clock, breezing through the quiz about inventions and resource development. Nine questions. Two extra credit. Eleven. I finish all eleven questions in nineteen minutes.

8:20

Eight plus two is ten minus eight is two. OK. Eight divided by two is four times eight is thirty-two minus eight is twenty-four minus eight is sixteen minus eight is eight minus two is six.

The numbers spin in my head.

"Eight twenty-one, people. Time's up." We pass our papers forward.

8:21

Eight plus two is ten plus one is eleven. OK. I watch the clock until it's 8:21 and 59 seconds, then turn my back to it.

Tick-tock.

It's like the tree-in-the-forest thing. If I can convince myself the clock isn't there, then I don't have to look at it. I don't have to think about the numbers. Then my mind can rest.

Math class can be a fucking nightmare.

I don't turn around for the rest of the period, even when somebody throws a balled-up paper at me. It ricochets off my desk onto the floor behind me. I hear giggles and Tanya's soft voice. "Pick it up," she purrs.

I feel a familiar stirring and concentrate on Ramón the Chihuahua and blue-painted claws. It's easier to imagine that when I look at her. But she has one of those husky voices that chicks usually have on the Spice Channel. And that's hot. Really hot.

Chihuahua Ramón. Chihuahua Ramón.

I don't pick up the note. I don't have time to turn around and get stuck on the clock. Plus it's about the most archaic way of sending notes ever. Can't she just text me?

I sigh and rub my temples, trying to semiconcentrate on Mr. Adams's lecture about American industrial economy blah blah blah.

During nutrition, I dodge the courtyard frenzy and hide out near my locker, gulping down Mom's turkey sandwich, skimming through our assigned chapter in *East of Eden*. Mera walks down the hall toward me, hugging her violin case to her chest. I shove my nose into the book.

I look for the words to—what's the word? *Transpire*. Yeah. Transpire through her skin and fill the hallway. I bang on the side of my head. Christ.

"Hey, Mera," I say, not looking up.

"Crazy morning."

"Yep." Don't look. Don't look. Bad luck.

I can feel her standing over me. Goddamnit. What did I say? What if she knows about me? I clear my throat. "Do you wanna at least sit down? You're hovering."

"You're in front of my locker." Her voice is flat, detached.

"Oh. Yeah. Um, sorry." I move over and she takes out some books, pulling out *East of Eden*, reading aloud. Steinbeck's words bounce off the lockers.

I sigh. Relieved.

"You are one of the rare people who can separate your observation from your preconception. You see what is, where most people see what they expect," she says. Then she repeats it, saying it just a little louder.

I look up and regret it instantly, because I can't stop staring into her eyes. Hazel with flecks of gold. But like one of those store mannequins. Because her hair is so pale, it looks like she has no lashes, like Kasey's dolls when she was a baby. Kasey used to pluck the lashes.

I'm not usually into the makeup thing, but I think Mera should use mascara.

"Huh?" I finally say, pulling my eyes away, staring at the floor and its zigzag design. Blue pentagons. White tiles. The hallway is a perfect geometrical symmetry of color and shapes. I like this hallway the most. It makes the most sense. I stare until the lines of color blur, then get sharp again. Seventeen times.

"Page one hundred sixty-one. I like that line." Mera's voice cuts through my thoughts.

"Sure," I say. "Maybe." *One sixty-one. Six plus one is seven minus one is six. No. Six times one is six plus one is seven. OK.* I skip to page 161 and find the line: *You are one of the rare people who can separate your observation from your preconception. You see what is, where most people see what they expect.* "What is," I mutter, and think about Mera playing violin or running seven hours straight. That's real, right?

And the magic that sweeps away the sticky webs that cover my frontal lobe? The magic. Is that real?

I shrug it off and take another bite of my sandwich and

try to chew quiet. Hearing people eat sends Mom over the edge, so we've become masters at great silences at the table. No chips. And no pudding. She hates that *squish, squish* sound.

One, two . . . seven, swallow. And again. Left side, right side. Balance. There's time. Always.

"You, um, want to sit down?" I ask.

She moves to sit down, then stops. "What? The Great Jake lowers himself to my level? Does *Magic Martin, the M&M*, want to be seen sitting next to UNICEF?"

"Ouch," I say. "I don't figure your orchestra-slash-band-slash-ultramarathon friends are too into my soccer accomplishments. So any reputation ruining will be bilateral."

"Touché," she says, and laughs. She sits down—her stick-figure arms and legs collapsing at my side. She smells like gingerbread cookies. My stomach growls. "It's a good book," she says. She has a nice voice. I offer her half my sandwich and she pushes it away. "Vegetarian," she says. "Not a pesca vegetarian or vegan. More lacto-no-ovo vegetarian."

"Huh?"

"I eat dairy, no eggs though. Not into scrambled pre-embryos."

"Thanks for the visual," I say.

"Call it culinary consciousness."

"Sure. Whatever." I swallow another bite of turkey sandwich, kind of relieved I'm not that socially, or food, conscious. "So that's what the Stormtrooper getup was all about this morning?"

She nods.

"Wow. What do your parents think about the vegetarian thing?" On top of owning Hartman Meats on Carson Street, Mera's dad is one of those champion big-game hunters, and half their house is decorated with stuffed animal heads. One of them is even an African antelope. She has four big brothers who smell like flanks of steak. Major carnivores.

"Well, at first I tried to hide it. But you know how hard it is to hide something like that?"

I clear my throat. "I can imagine." I think for a bit. "So when'd you tell them? I mean, how?" If she told her big secret, maybe I could tell mine. But what do I have to tell? It's not like anything's *really* wrong with me.

"When our dog, Max, choked on a chicken bone I fed to him during dinner and died, I told them."

"*Uff,*" I say, and try to stifle a laugh. "Sorry. Don't mean to laugh. That's, um, so sad."

"The irony is not lost on me," she says. "It was a long time ago, anyway. Nobody can keep a secret that big for long. It's bound to leak out."

"How do you still work at your dad's? Isn't that against some kind of lacto-no-ovo vegetarian principle?"

"Yep. But my dad feels like I need a reminder of where my clothes, violin, and everything else he does for us financially comes from, so every now and again, I get to work in the shop. This morning was one of those days I needed that valuable reminder. So to answer your question: They think I'm weird."

"That sucks."

She laughs. "What about you?"

I look at her. "What about me what?"

"Do you think I'm weird?"

"A little." I nod.

"Thanks."

I shrug. "Well, you asked."

"I did."

"You still watch the Home Shopping Network when you can't sleep?" I ask.

She cocks her head to the side. "Good memory."

I blush. "Yeah. I guess."

"Nah. Now it's the Travel Channel. Or I play violin." Dark rings circle her eyes.

The notes from her violin music form in my head—her latest work. I wish I knew the name of it, that she'd play it here in the hallway. Now.

I wonder if she knows how good she is. I almost tell her.

"There's gotta be more than Carson City, you know?" she says.

I shrug. I'm not one of those get-out-of-Carson City

types, and next year I'll be sent away to some fucking college, probably end up rooming with the biggest slob on the planet who doesn't keep his clock wound. My stomach burns, and I shake the thought away.

What if I can do college correspondence?

What if I could do my whole life correspondence?

I'm seriously wacko.

"Out of Carson?" I say. "Half the time I don't even want to leave my room. But Anthony Bourdain's show is good." I can't believe I admitted that to her, and I hold my breath.

She raises her eyebrows. "Oh yeah, traveling and eating with a cynical bastard."

Exhale.

"Two o'clock a.m.," we both say. She smiles. She looks pretty when she smiles. Real pretty.

"You still don't sleep either?" she asks.

"Good memory," I say, and shrug. "Just lots on my mind, I guess." Fucking numbers.

"I guess."

She pulls out a sandwich. Sprouts and mushy white things stick out of the sides. It smells like onions and old socks. She takes a big bite. "Want some?" she asks between gulps.

"Not a chance."

She laughs. We're quiet. And I feel okay. Like her silence isn't bursting with ugly words. Like we can just be, and having Mera sit next to me is a good thing.

My mind is still.

When we were little, Mera, Luc, and I built a fort in Luc's backyard. And we'd all hang out there on Saturday mornings just doing kid shit. Like nothing in the world mattered. Mera would bring her violin and we'd invent songs. Luc would be lead 'cause he's a really good singer. I'd write most of the lyrics with Mera and sing backup. He'd *shit* if anybody knew about the singing part.

It all seemed easier back then. I guess when we're little pretending is okay. But when we grow up, pretending is more like lying. I don't know.

"Remember the song game?" I ask.

She looks up from the book and nods. "Yeah. I haven't thought about that for a while."

"Today's category: country-western song titles for every profession. I'll start with butcher: 'Stand By Your Ham' or 'Go-Lean.'" I half laugh and turn to Mera's pale-eyed stare. "Well?" I ask.

"Jake, we're not twelve anymore, you know." She tucks pale strands of hair behind her ear.

I return to the hallway, the way things *are*, kind of wishing for then. "Yeah. I know. I just thought—"

She shrugs and goes back to reading.

I think about the line from the book again: *You are one of the rare people who can separate your observation from your preconception. You see what is, where most people see what they expect.* "It's not about what's real and what we expect to see," I mutter. "I think it's the doubting, the wondering about it all. Like how nothing makes sense unless—I dunno. Always doubting, wondering. What if—"

Why don't I just shut up? Now. Christ.

Mera closes her book, picks at a hangnail, and waits. "What if what?" she asks.

What if the numbers aren't prime? Now that sounds crazy. I rub my eyes and pull my fingers through my hair. I know I've said too much, like a little part of me just hangs there in the hall. But it's just Mera. UNICEF. Ultramarathon Mera, who has been categorized as social untouchable since seventh grade.

She doesn't matter. She's not supposed to, anyway.

"What if" doesn't matter. It's a kid game—a stupid thing I do. So I tuck that piece of me back inside—way down deep where nobody will see it. The magic is protected. Everything is right again.

"Jake?" She looks at me hard—a long, blinkless stare. "I mean, this morning at the shop, during the rally. You seem—"

Blink, I think. *Just blink.* And I count.

She breaks my concentration saying, "The doubting?"

Blink. Blink.

"Christ, Mera, it's nothing," I say. The peaceful bubble

fissures and explodes, and I feel like my chest is being compressed again; my airways are constricting. The tingling begins and explodes into my brain. I rub my temples and push on my forehead.

I've been caught. She knows.

Fucking Mera. I tap my pencil on the book and look back down the hallway at the patterns.

"Do you talk about it?" she asks. "I mean, not with me. Do you, um, talk to Luc about this stuff?"

Yeah, sure. *Hey, Luc, did you know that it can take me up to two hours to leave the house some days because the numbers don't work?* That's exactly what I want to talk to the ever-macho, ever-okay Luc about.

I shove my books into my backpack. I can't hear her words over the hammering in my ears. My breath quickens, so I count, bringing it back, keeping it cool. Tuck. Tuck. Tuck. *Put the piece away.*

The bell rings and I jump up, relieved. I throw my backpack over my shoulder and hurry down the hallway toward English, feeling her eyes bore into the back of my neck. I guess I could've waited for her. Walked together. Sometimes I feel like a total asshole.

But she breaks the magic. I need to stay focused for Saturday. I don't have time to get caught up in what used to be and what is now. I can't go back. I can't look forward. I just need now. That's all.

I can feel Mera's stare—like the prickle of hot sun on the back of my neck. I scratch it away.

What if she knows about me?

I shake my head. No way. *Focus. Just focus. The game. Getting to class on time. Focus.*

I walk away, leaving her again.

TWENTY-NINE THE FUTURE

Thursday, 2:15 p.m.

Two fifteen. Two plus one is three plus five is eight minus five is three. OK.

Before practice Coach calls me aside, holding a copy of the tardy-notice letter Dad showed me this morning. I want to tell him he should photocopy it and send it to nine people or else his balls will fall off or something equally horrible if he breaks the chain. *Keep the tardy chain going.*

But I like Coach too much to be a total smart-ass. And those are only thoughts.

I pause and stare at him, waiting for a reaction.

Good. I didn't say it out loud.

Just thoughts.

Coach shows me the letter. "Martin, you can't afford to be late again. Take this seriously."

Tick-tock, tick-tock.

I nod, my body itching to get out there and run. Get the release. When I'm out there, the spiders disappear.

"Jake," he says, "Principal Vaughn doesn't mess around. He's here and ready to prove a point—*no* exceptions. Eight tardies and you're benched—state final on Saturday or not. Don't mess it up."

"I won't, Coach." Only one day of school left before the final game anyway. I only have to be on time one more day. That won't be hard.

Coach is still talking, so I start counting his words, my mind racing to keep up.

"You're the best team player we've got. Scouts . . . college scholarships . . . teamwork . . . Martin, are you listening?"

"A hundred seventy-three."

"A hundred seventy-three what?" Coach asks.

Numbers. Words. *One hundred seventy-three. One plus seven is eight plus three is eleven. OK.*

"Okay. Just—yeah, I'm there, Coach. You can count on me."

"We need you *here*," Coach says. "Now."

"Is there any other place?"

He smiles. "Okay then," he says. "Get out there and

let's have a good practice."

We group up seven-on-seven to play short-sided, practicing skills, going over plays. The fog melts away, the itching disappears. The field is a crisp, glossy photo—the kind in which every blade of grass is in macrofocus. Everything is clear, and the only thing I have to worry about is getting around a few guys who don't know their asses from their elbows, tripping over themselves to stop me.

But they can't.

It's a dance. I flick the ball around Kalleres, push past Keller. Diaz comes forward. He's the best fucking goalie in Nevada—but not good enough. So I lob the ball over a stunned Diaz, who's stranded on the edge of the area, prepared for a power kick. It floats into the net like it was filled with helium, pausing in the air before dropping to the ground with the earth's gravitational pull.

It's magic out here. This is my fairy tale, my Neverland. No tick. No tock. Just me, the ball, and the goal.

After Saturday, it has to end. Because Saturday is the magic number three. Everything I've done has built up to this because it's my thirteenth year of school, third championship, the end of the cycle, the beginning of real life. We're playing *the* game on Saturday, November 5. Saturday is the seventh day of the week. November is the eleventh month. *Seven plus eleven is eighteen plus five is twenty-three.*

The game is at three o'clock in the afternoon.

Perfect.

When we win, everything will be okay. The spiders will go away, the shimmering white light of migraines and drilling pain in my temples will disappear. Saturday will be magic.

I'll get to keep that magic with me forever because I did it right.

We'll all live happily ever after.

"Practice is over!" Coach hollers across the field. "Give Diaz a break already."

"Three more," I say between breaths, and power in three more goals—left, right, left. All get past Diaz. He doesn't even try. "C'mon, man," I say.

"I'm wrecked, Martin. Christ, it's like you're some kind of goddamned Energizer bunny." I pull him up. "Nice scoop back there. I never expected that. *Mierda*." He pulls off his goalie gloves and almost bowls me over with the stench.

"Can't you wash those things?"

"Not all season, M&M. These babies get me through the game."

"Probably because they can block on their own," I say.

"Dude, why do you think we win?"

"Magic," I say, laughing. Diaz smirks. Magic. We all have a little bit of it.

Luc sleeps with his uniform on the night before a game.

Keller never washed the socks he wore in our first championship win three years ago and has them buried in his backyard under a weird shrine he has to Lionel Messi—an autographed soccer ball he got when he saw Messi play in Barcelona.

And I have the numbers.

Diaz and I limp to where the rest of the team sprawls on the grass. Coach claps me on the back and turns to the team. "He hasn't been a starter for three years for nothin'."

"Kiss-ass," mutters Luc.

I shrug and lie down, staring up at the blue sky. One, two, three, four clouds. Then two blend together and there are three.

Magic.

Coach is talking about Bishop Gorman's offense. Their right forward is pretty amazing, being scouted for UCLA's soccer program. Big deal. It's all about the team. It's all about the numbers. Eleven players making magic.

For some reason I'm thinking about Mera. Not in an I-wanna-get-in-her-pants way. Just in an I-wish-we-still-hung-out way. Maybe I'll join her ultramarathon club. I'll need some sport after this year's championship win.

I doze to the sound of his voice; the prickly grass blades tickle the nape of my neck. Every muscle in my body relaxes and my mind is at rest. This is how I'll feel forever when the stuff that gets my brain all funky disappears—floats away.

Win number three.

Coach says, with a tinge of pride in his voice, "Scouts. I've gotten several calls. College scouts are coming out here this Saturday to look at a couple of you. This is a big game—a big opportunity. Big future."

I close my eyes tighter. Coach says *future* like it's the most important word we'll ever hear. That's a total geezer thing. "Future, future, future." Maybe because they have less of one. I dunno. Parents, teachers, and Coach are so fucking stuck on tomorrow.

I can't even get past now.

"M&M! M&M!" someone chants.

I open my eyes. The sun is already low in the sky and there's a late-afternoon chill in the air. I shiver.

"Nah. They're here for Luc," I say. "And definitely Grundy and Kalleres."

Luc won't look at me. We know they're not here for him. He's good. Carson City good. Maybe Nevada good. Not college good.

Coach clears his throat. "Duke. UCLA. Maryland."

Some guys whistle.

"No shit," Luc says, and starts pulling grass from the field, his jaw tense.

"No shit," Coach says, and clears his throat, mumbling, "Excuse my language."

After a brief silence Coach says, "You're all great players.

All of you. But I don't want anybody being a hotshot out there. Do your job on the field like you have every game this past year."

"In other words, stay out of Martin's way," Diaz says, and laughs. "Fucking scoop. Never saw that coming."

There is no I *in team.*

"See you tomorrow." Coach looks at me. "On time, Martin. Saturday's too important for the team." *You,* though, is implied. Saturday is my future. Ninety minutes of my life on a field will decide everything—college for Coach and Dad.

Peace for me—a weightlessness and calm I only feel out here. And I have to make sure it lasts a lifetime.

Saturday I can't screw it up.

We stand up and stretch. Practice wasn't so hard. We're just tired from having to condition at dark-thirty in the morning.

Luc shrugs and mutters, "Asshole doesn't even care about scouts. *Guevón.*" It's an affront to him that his nut best friend is better at soccer. He once told me that being Colombian meant he had the right to be better because the soccer fans down there were for real—not some white-collared assholes following the latest sports trend. In Colombia it's do or die.

I'm just glad he's not Argentinian or I'd probably be crucified by the Maradonians, Year of Their God, AB 51.

I close my eyes and try to recapture that moment before everybody got all hung up on the future. But it's gone now and the spiders are working their way up my neck again—mad web spinners trapping all my words, fogging my thoughts.

I keep my eyes shut until I feel Luc kicking on my side. "Let's go out with Tanya and Amy before dinner. Maybe to Comma Coffee or something." Luc pulls me up and we head to the locker room and shower up.

Amy and Tanya are waiting for us in the parking lot. I can't help but think about Ren Höek. "Luc," I venture. "Does Tanya remind you of *something*?"

I do a mental list of famous Chihuahuas because I don't think Luc's ever seen Ramón, Sarah Merckley's little rat dog. He's gotta know Ren from *Ren and Stimpy* and Mojo the diarrhea dog from *Transformers*.

Luc elbows me. "Yeah. Tanya Reese. You know what they say about Reese's." He smirks.

"What? It's more than a mouthful?"

"No, *guevón*, that's Whatchamacallit. A Reese's is even better."

"Yeah. You would probably know."

He shakes his head. "Unfortunate last name, however appropriate."

We both laugh. I squint, trying to picture Chihuahua Tanya and me getting horizontal. Maybe if I just close my eyes and listen to her talk. That would be hot.

Just then Mera walks past us, her violin case banging against her thigh.

"Holy 'Colors of the Wind,' Pocahontas," Tanya says.

Mera's wearing these worn-out boots with fringes, a mini jean skirt—real mini—and a heavy wool sweater.

Tanya makes an obnoxious Indian sound like in those Old West movies.

I cringe and stand away, trying not to be with them, but trying not to look like I'm not wanting to be with them. Pretending again.

Tanya continues, "The other day she refused to partner up with me in class, saying I didn't have enough EFAs in my diet to feed my brain, so my work is substandard. Then she handed me an avocado. Like, ewww."

I stifle a laugh. Mera's the only high-school loner/ orchestra geek/nerd I know who has a superiority complex.

"As if anybody else in class wants to partner up with her." Tanya's still fuming. But Mera only did in class what Tanya and every other double-X chromosome in the school does to her every day at school. Treat her like crap. She hums the presidential march and says, "Voted Most Forgettable Senior at Carson High."

Amy laughs. Then Tanya laughs. Hollow. Mean.

I try to blow it off, but it bugs me. Why do chicks have to do that? I look at Tanya again and all I see is ugly. Plus the whole idea of being voted Most Forgettable makes somebody unforgettable, undermining the entire insult. But I don't say anything.

Maybe Mera's right and she doesn't have enough calories to keep her brain functioning. Her collarbone juts out like a shelf with a ripple of ribs that fan like a grooved shell below it. I don't think you're supposed to see somebody's ribs from the front. Suddenly all I want to do is fill her up with protein smoothies from Comma Coffee.

My sympathy doesn't linger, because now Amy and Tanya are talking about how weird Mera smells.

"Enough," I say. "Just. Enough."

Tanya and Amy stop laughing and do that oh-my-God gaping-mouth stare chicks are really good at. I guess I broke some kind of code or something.

Mera's cheeks are blotchy red in the cold wind. "Mera!" I holler out to her.

"What?" She turns to me, throwing her backpack in the passenger seat of her dad's old meat van. She has a bumper sticker that says I'VE CHAFED IN PLACES THAT YOU'VE NEVER HEARD OF with a picture of a worn-out pair of running shoes on it.

We've had lots of laughs about the bumper sticker. Now I feel pretty bad about that.

"Enjoy Bourdain!" I wave.

She smiles. "You too," she says.

She opens the door and scoots in, rolling down the window. When she drives by us, she waves at me. I feel like I have a little piece of me back—something I've been missing.

"Like, are you guys *friends*?" Amy asks.

Before I can answer, Luc says, "We all grew up together." He runs his fingers through his damp hair.

Amy says, "Sorry. I didn't know she was your friend."

"Should it make a difference?" I say.

Tanya and Amy look away. Tanya scuffs her shoe across the pavement.

"Shit, are we gonna stand here all day doing the After-School Special thing and staring at the asphalt or get some juice? I'm freezing." Luc flashes his Colgate smile and rolls his eyes at me. "Chicks are like that," he'd say. He'd know. He's hitting a different one every other weekend.

I clear my throat. "Let's go," I say, forcing myself to smile at Tanya, trying to look past her words even though they're still hanging out there in the cold air.

She says them. We all think them. Maybe she's okay and we're all hypocrites. Christ, I don't know.

"Yeah, let's go," Amy says. We pile into Luc's car and head to Comma Coffee.

I open my wallet. "Ah, Christ. I don't have cash."

Luc shrugs. "It's on me." Amy titters and does some kind of swoony thing she probably saw in a chick flick.

Admittedly, it looks pretty hot. I glance at Tanya and she's smiling at me.

Luc looks in the rearview mirror and says, "I've got you covered too, Tanya."

She smiles and blushes.

Shit. He's doing that Latin gentleman thing. Tomorrow, though, he'll hit me up for my drink, Tanya's, and probably make me chip in for gas. Cheap-ass. He looks at me through the rearview mirror and grins, mouthing, *"Guevón."*

Comma Coffee is packed. We find a table in the back corner. Tanya orders black coffee. Amy, too. Luc and I each have extra-large caramel-pump caffeine-blasters. I try to coax Tanya into eating a bagel. Anything. She smiles, bats her eyes like Amy did earlier, but they're so fucking big I swear I feel a breeze coming from her lashes and hear a weird, winglike whooshing sound. She sips on the bitter black coffee.

Luc, Amy, and Tanya talk about the game, school, pep rallies, winter dances. About nothing. I nod. It's like I'm on autopilot, just needing to get to my room, someplace safe where I won't have to listen to anybody anymore. The pain in my head is constant, and I don't even try to keep the spiders away anymore. Sometimes the dull throbbing feels better when I let it happen.

Talk, talk, talk until they bore themselves into silence. Plus Luc has to be home by dinner, leaving him limited hookup time with Amy. He kicks me under the table, and I guzzle my drink. I can literally feel the blood vessels expanding in my head, the stabbing pain of electrified nerves. I grip my head between my hands. "Brain freeze. Brain freeze. Jesus Christ!"

Everybody laughs. I do too, because it feels great to have a headache like this—one that will go away without numbers or time or counting. It feels so *normal*.

"You can take the caffeine-blasters to go, you know," Luc says. "Geez. I can't take you *anywhere*." But he's laughing. This is something he can relate to.

"Yeah. And have Dad see me with this. No thanks."

Luc drives me home first. I avoid making eye contact with Tanya, which is pretty hard considering her eyes take up half her face. Luc clears his throat. I'm cutting into his feel-up time.

Tick-tock.

"See you," I say to Tanya, and jump out of the car, dodging what looked like a major going-for-the-landing open-lip pucker. *God, I'm an asshole. Who wouldn't want some of that?*

I turn to the streetlight. It doesn't sputter. I sigh, tap the flamingo, and open the door.

Here's Jakey. I feel my eyes get buggy.

Christ. I've got to lay off the caffeine.

THIRTY-ONE PAYING DEBTS

Thursday, 6:19 p.m.

Six nineteen. Six times nine is fifty-four minus one is fifty-three. OK.

The table is set. The house smells like heated Styrofoam and boiled meat. I hear the beep of the microwave. Dad puts a plastic plate with plastic food in front of Kasey. She carefully scoops out the food on her plate so the mashed potatoes and peas are parallel to each other with the supposed turkey breast on top. It looks a little like a shrine.

Dad smiles at Kasey and sits next to her. I feel like I'm interrupting something. Like sitting down will shatter the normalness.

I don't belong. One foot in, one foot out.

"Hey," I say, dropping my backpack by the clock. "I'm starved."

Dad motions to the microwave—billions of invisible waves bouncing off each other to heat the plate of food. Pots bubble on the stovetop. The oven has two pans baking. The rice cooker, Crock-Pot, and vegetable steamer are plugged in. Everything else smells better than the microwaved plastic.

It beeps and I take it out, plopping the tray on the table, sitting across from Kasey. When I peel off the plastic, the steam burns my fingers, "Shit!"

Dad looks up, glowering.

"Excuse me. So, um, what's with the Food Network here?"

"Mom didn't put the meat away. It defrosted. Dad and I have been cooking since he got home because you can't refreeze meat or you'll die of Ebola. We've prepared pot roast, pork chops, ground chuck, chicken, beef stew, pork sausage, and . . ." She looks at Dad.

"Turhamken."

"Yeah. But we didn't cook the turhamken. It's just in the fridge. When everything's done and cooled, we'll freeze it. Then for the next month, every meal we eat will be defrosted and nuked." Kasey forks her peas, one by one. "And you wonder why I prefer Papa Murphy's."

Dad smiles when he looks at Kasey, like she's the thing he's done right.

"Where's Mom?" I ask, trying to swallow the powdery potatoes.

"In bed," Kasey says.

"Oh."

"Since, like, before I got home."

I look down at my plate—the pea juice running into the potatoes. "Oh."

"Mr. Hartman phoned," Dad says.

I wait for the blow. But that's the thing. He doesn't say anything else. He doesn't go into some kind of speech about fiscal responsibility—economy of time and money. It's like making a fist but never throwing the punch. The tension is always here, just never the release.

Growing up, Luc only ever got the release before his dad left. Mera and I used to help him pretend that it was all right. And I wish they could help me pretend today.

If you can't see blood, it doesn't hurt.

Inhale. Wait for Saturday. After Saturday everything will be right.

Time stands still until Dad continues to talk. Kasey's waiting, her fork suspended over the last few peas on her plate. Four.

I look away from her plate and stare down at mine.

"Mr. Hartman called. Something about you and Mera

getting trapped in a walk-in freezer?" Dad says.

"Yeah. It's no big deal. Some old guy was there and opened the door up for us." I steady myself against the dining-room table, squeezing its edge so nobody can see how much I'm trembling. *Shake it off. Fuck.*

"And if the old guy hadn't been there?" Dad asks.

What if?

Dad plays too.

"You two could've gotten hurt. You could've died."

I look at Dad. He looks angry. Or is that concern?

"You're not gonna sue or anything?" I can't imagine Dad doing the whole lawsuit thing.

"No. But I'm not happy with the situation and Mr. Hartman knows it. There's absolutely no reason for you to be doing their job. I understand," he continues, "why you were running late. But I don't understand why you didn't tell me."

Exhale. "Yeah. No big deal." I almost tell him how freaked out I was, how it reminded me of the night Mom left us alone. I just want him to be my dad sometimes. "I'll tell you next time."

"There won't be a next time, Jacob."

"Yeah. You know what I mean."

Dad nods. We eat the rest of dinner in silence, crumpling up our used trays in the garbage. Kasey rinses her plate off and puts it in the dishwasher. Dad ruffles her hair, checking on the various food concoctions. The steam fogs the windows.

"We'll take care of the rest of the food, Dad. So you can get to work in the garage," I say.

Dad looks at me.

I nod.

He pulls three timers off the counter and sets them on the table. It's like listening to a time bomb countdown symphony—except nothing will explode in the end.

Dad heads to the garage, leaving Kasey and me on cafeteria duty. We pull out our homework. For a while there's nothing but the sound of our pencils scribbling across the page.

Tick-tock, tick-tock.

The timers are out of sync. I pick them up and shove them in the couch cushions.

Kasey stares at me.

"They're distracting," I say.

"You're so weird."

"Because I don't like the sound of the timers?"

"Weird-o," she mutters, showing incredible restraint not tapping into her "crackers" category.

"Yesterday, we established my weird is mysteriously cool," I say, and cringe because I can hear the shrill note in my voice. Being me is *not* cool, and I think Kasey must know that. How can she not?

Plus since yesterday, I can't get rid of the webs—it's harder to, anyway. I just need a few days and things will go back to normal. It just hasn't been this bad for a while. I need Saturday, the game, the win. Three. Perfect number three.

"Now it's just irritating," she says.

I swallow and say, "K, I'm just kind of distracted, I guess."

"Whatever," she says. "Mr. Count-to-a-Thousand-Hold-Your-Breath-Before-Leaving. It's not like Dad asks that much of you. It's really shit you spent the grocery money on some toothpick chick at a burger joint. I've been stuck cooking since three o'clock this afternoon because said groceries defrosted."

"Mom said she'd put the meat away," I say.

"Yeah. Mom says a lot of things, doesn't she? Just like you."

"Sorry." I push my hair out of my eyes and tuck it behind my ears. "Really. I am." She can't even begin to imagine how sorry I am.

I think she can tell I'm pretty run down because she sits next to me. "So who's the lucky girl?"

"What girl?"

"Burger-joint-grocery-money girl."

"Tanya Reese."

"Tanya Reese? Tan-yeah Reese?"

"What's that supposed to mean?"

"She's . . . " Kase says.

"She's what?" I ask.

"You know. Like, do you *know* her?"

"*Know* her? In that biblical knowing way? Or in the way we were in Mr. Nutting's fourth-grade class together. She used to sell Girl Scout cookies," I say, surprised I'm defending Tanya.

"Well, what kind of badge is she working toward now? Virgin crusaders? Are you her last good deed?"

"Kase." I hold up my hand. "Don't."

She knows she's crossed the line. "Sorry."

"Fine." I close my books.

"You got lots of homework?" Kase asks, breaking the silence.

"It can wait. It's for Monday. So tell me about your day," I say after swallowing down the knot that lodged in my throat, trying to bring the routine back.

Kasey complains about Mr. Gorski's comb-over and how her friend Lisa has a crush on me which she's totally pissed about because that's not cool and breaks some kind of code the group has written up and signed. Then she mentions this party Mario Gomez is throwing this weekend. Mario's place is famous for a massive loft upstairs, four or five storage closets, perfect for getting laid.

"No." There's no way I'm taking Kasey to the closest

thing to a teenage brothel for her first rager.

"It's for maintenance, Jake. Really. It's not like I'm going to drink or anything. Plus it'll be fun. I'm going with Jessica and Marcy. I'll take my cell. C'mon. You've gotta back me up on this one."

"No." I shake my head. "Not at Mario's."

"It's just a stupid party," she insists. "The *whole school* is going."

"I can't be worried about that kind of shit this weekend. Another weekend. And I'll go with you all. Just to hang out. But not now. I've been to parties up there, and it's not a cool scene." I haven't actually been to parties there. But I've heard enough about them to know Kase shouldn't go.

"You *owe* me."

One of the buzzers dings from under the couch cushion. "Which one is this for?" I ask, pulling it out.

"Pot roast," she says, grabbing some oven mitts. I open the oven and pull out the rack so Kasey can grab the pan. She places it on a trivet and comes back to the table. "So? Are you going to cover for me or be the total asshole brother of the century?"

"Those are my options?"

She glares and I wonder what crackers brand she has designated for me. Like all this hiding I do—all this sneaking around isn't even sneaking. It's just everybody else not seeing what is, just what they want to see. Does Kasey see?

Does Mera?

Who else?

"I know you do a ton for me." I clear my throat. "I know you help me out. But *not* this weekend."

"It's not like I need your permission." She pouts.

"Like hell you don't. It's not gonna happen. Period. Not at Mario's, okay?"

"Thanks a lot, Jake."

I put my arm around her and ignore her protests. "Not this weekend. I promise I'll cover for you next weekend. I'll *go* next weekend. And you can even invite Lisa." I smirk.

"Asshole." She punches my arm.

I laugh. "You're all I've got that matters, okay?"

"Yeah," she mutters. "Flattery isn't gonna cut it today. I'll go to the next party. No matter what."

"I'll take you."

"You won't let me down?"

"Not this time." I hope not, anyway. I'm always trying to make up for the things I do wrong, chasing time, fixing the past.

"At least you're honest." Another buzzer goes off, and we pull out a pan of pork chops.

She yawns.

"I'll take care of everything down here in the land of the Food Network. Go watch TV or something."

"Now you're just trying to make up for being asshole

brother of the universe."

"Thought it was century."

"Time and place," Kasey says. "Of the universe this century. Just don't let the stew overcook, okay? There's nothing worse than eating rubber for dinner."

When she goes, I arrange the timers on the tables, my eyes darting between them, fixing the numbers. One by one, they ding, and I spend the rest of the evening listening to the metronomic *tick-tick-tick* of the windup timer until its hammer bangs against a tinny bell. I turn off the stove and wait for the food to cool. I lay my head on the table and close my eyes, already wishing it was Saturday so I could get it all over with.

It's after ten when everything is finally cool and packed away. I bring the food out to the garage, to the deep freeze, where Dad sits at his workbench, carving something on the front of a newly sanded chest. Wood shavings curl, dropping to the floor like petals. His back is curved over the bench in an arc.

I place the food in the freezer and step away silently, leaving him in the sanctuary of his garage. Kasey's gone to bed. The only sounds are the tick of the grandfather clock and the sighs of the wind on the windows. I walk upstairs and head to the cocoon of my room so I don't break the shell of silence.

Friday, 2:23 a.m.

And one second. Two twenty-three. Two plus two is four plus three is seven. OK. Two minus two is zero plus three is three. OK. Two times twenty-three is forty-six minus two is forty-four minus three is forty-one. OK. Fifty-five, fifty-six.

I turn from the clock. Just as I mentally count, it turns to 2:24.

My watch is on the nightstand next to the clock.

I feel like I'm forgetting something. When that happens, it's like everything gets stuck—the cogs on the clock stop until my mind grasps what it needs and can start to work again.

When I close my eyes, I see numbers imprinted on my lids, so I rework them, calculate, add, subtract.

Fuckit.

I get up and take down three clocks from the closet, putting the boxes back and shutting the door. Two need batteries.

The room feels like it's getting smaller, like the ticks on my watch pound in my ears. I pull open the window and pop the screen off, sticking my head outside, sucking in the night air, squeezing my eyes so that all the stars blur into one.

Count the lights.

That always helps. It breaks the numbers. Going for a walk, counting the lights in houses. The muscle in my right thigh spasms.

So fucking tired.

I don't want to freeze my balls off wandering around west Carson City counting houses that have lights on, so I flick on the TV, leaving the window open.

The clocks are lined up under the window.

Just in case.

Just in case?

Bourdain's in Uzbekistan.

I've seen this one before and turn on the captions so Dad doesn't hear. I wonder if Mera's watching it.

I bet she is.

And that actually makes me feel better, knowing I'm not the only asshole in the world that can't sleep.

The red numbers glow at me from my bedside clock and I finally turn it away, facing the window after I've gone through all the prime numbers up to seven hundred thirty-three three times to match the time when I took off my watch and shoved it into my backpack this morning. I fall asleep during the part when Bourdain is baby shopping, carrying around a crib and blanket.

They rush into the room, flicking on the light and ripping open the blinds to predawn's purple-black sky. "SURPRISE!"

"Get out of bed, Martin. We're being hijacked for breakfast." Luc stands at the foot of the bed in his pajamas, surrounded by cheerleaders. He shrugs and mouths, "I had no idea." He half smiles. "C'mon, man. It's time to break tradition. Loosen up a little." He's wearing the same T-shirt he wore yesterday and smells like it. Black stubble dots his chin. Not many guys at school actually *need* to shave.

Luc does.

It's supposed to be tomorrow—the day of the game. They always do the surprise breakfast thing the day of the game. And that way I'm prepared for them to come. That way things stay the way they're supposed to.

That way, we win.

Luc runs his fingers through his bed-head hair. "C'mon, Martin. Lighten up. It's not really a big deal."

It is.

I rub my eyes and look for the clock. It fell to the floor, coming unplugged when they poured into the room.

Unplugged.

Fuck.

No time.

I yank my watch off the nightstand. It's stopped. I forgot to wind it. See, windup watches are better because batteries go dead. So you never have to worry about your watch not working.

As long as you wind it.

Shit.

I slap it on my wrist even though it's stopped.

Time. Has. Stopped. The hands don't move.

What day is it?

Friday.

Winding days: Thursdays and Mondays.

Yesterday I didn't wind my watch.

And now time has stopped.

Tick-tock, tick-tock. I put the watch to my ear, aching to hear that sound, but nothing comes.

I look around at the faces surrounding my bed. Kasey pushes her way through the crowd and tries to get everybody to go away. "Let him get ready," she says. "Just give him five minutes." God, I love Kase.

One of the cheerleaders pats Kasey's head like she's some kind of puppy and says, "Oh so cute," then shoves her aside.

Dad and Mom huddle together in their robes. Dad smiles. "It's almost impossible to surprise this guy. I don't know how you pulled it off."

Mom looks tired, distracted. She leans closer into Dad, like this is a home invasion. I wonder if anybody else notices the quiver in her lips. I've got to get them out of here. I don't know if it's to spare Mom or to spare us the embarrassment of Mom.

Tanya tugs on my arm. "Let's go. We're going to the Nugget for a breakfast banquet." Everybody chants our soccer song—one we took from Manchester United.

> If you want to go to heaven when you die
> Keep the Carson High flag flying high;
> Get yourself a Senator bonnet;
> And put "F*** Bishop Gorman" on it;
> If you want to go to heaven when you die.

"Why *bonnet*?" Kase asked once.

"Because no other article of clothing rhymes with 'on it,'" I told her.

Nobody else at school cares. And three years ago, for

the final game, everybody showed up in bonnets. Now it's our soccer tradition at the school for home games. It's absolutely insane—like whatever Luc does, goes. "Power," Luc says. Luc's the guy who could weave gold out of air and get the president to wear the invisible clothes. It just doesn't make him a better soccer player.

"C'mon, Martin. I'm famished." Luc yanks me out of bed all the way, and the cheerleaders laugh. He leans into me. "Relax. It's not a big deal, okay?"

"Tighty whiteys!" They giggle.

I hurry and pull on a pair of sweats.

Out of order.

I need time—to work out the numbers. Then sock, sock, sweats, shirt, then shoes. I freeze, trying to find a way to reverse everything—make it all okay.

They're messing up the magic.

They shove me downstairs, blocking the grandfather clock, pushing me out the door before I can do anything the way I'm supposed to.

It's still too dark—a starless blackness.

I can't go.

I push my way toward the front door, my fingers brushing the flamingo's beak. I'm supposed to go back inside. Touch beak. Go inside. My fingers tingle. But they grab me and shove me down the walk.

The streetlight sputters.

I just need to stop. Stop. Breathe. Count. And get things okay.

Goddamned light. It shouldn't sputter.

I need to wait for the light.

Wait until dawn.

Start. Over.

My fingers start to burn. I touched the beak. I have to go inside.

Instead, I'm crammed in the back of someone's car with Tanya on my lap. The air is impregnated with the smell of overripe guava and tangy citrus—like the produce section of Supermercado Chalo on Sundays, where Luc's mom buys these funky tropical fruits. I breathe through my mouth but then taste the fruity air particles and have to swallow back the acidic bile that has worked its way up from my stomach. Tanya's hair tickles my nose; her bony ass digs into my thighs.

The car bounces down the road and squeals to a stop in the Nugget parking lot, and we spill out of the car just in time for me to gulp down the fresh morning air before Tanya's decomposing fruit-smelling hair makes me retch. I lean over, hands on knees, my palms burning against the fabric of my sweats. Webs are being woven in the back of my brain and work their way upward. It feels like my head is going to split in half.

Tanya tugs on my elbow. "Are you even listening to me, Jake?" she asks.

I look at her and nod. "Just give me a sec. Just a second." I squeeze my eyes shut and try to push away the pain, but the best I get to is a dull throb that I know won't go away for hours.

I need to get back home and start over. I can't eat here. Not like this. But before I can think through anything, Luc, Diaz, and some other guys grab me and start to chant:

> *If ever they are playing in your town,*
> *You must get to that soccer ground;*
> *Take a lesson and come on in,*
> *Soccer taught by Jake Martin;*
> *We love Jake!*
> *We love Jake!*
> *We love Jake!*

It's like their words are chiseling my skull while the spiders burrow deeper into my brain. If I can't control it, I'll be comatose for a week.

Walking into the Nugget is like walking into a time warp: smudgy mirrors, shitty lighting, and that underlying smoker smell that permeates from the burnt sienna–colored carpeting.

Banners and streamers hang from the rafters in the banquet hall. Everybody is decked out in blue and white. The band is set up near the stage, playing the Senators' fight song. The orchestra is next to them, sawing on their instruments. Mera looks bored, probably not amused by the fact she has to play something as mundane as the Senators' fight song on her precious strings.

I concentrate, though, on the movement of the bow pulling across the strings—trying to focus just on the sound that comes from Mera's violin. I've almost got it when a couple of guys jump on my back and start to chant again, breaking the music away.

I stagger to a chair. For a second everything goes black, so I shove my palms into my eyes and push real hard. It's like watching an electric storm when I do that—spider bodies frying on my brain, their fibrous webs trapping any rational thought.

Somebody claps me hard on the back and says, "Wake up, man. How can you sleep through *this*?"

I look up, and the veil of black lifts in time for me to see Luc staring at me. "*Guevón*," he mouths. The vein on his neck is pulsating. He looks at me not like I'm Jake but like I'm some kind of lab experiment in a petri dish.

There's a plate of steaming biscuits and gravy in front of me.

"Assmunch," I mouth back, and rub my eyes, acting like I'm zombie-tired and not a step from falling into wacko-land. *Keep it cool*, I think.

Luc cracks a smile, then is swallowed up by the rest of

the team, leaving me behind.

I exhale and search the room for a clock, finding a crooked-hanging one on the wall to the right. I cock my head to the side, but it still looks crooked; the floor has a Titanic slant, and I clutch the edge of the table so I won't go careening to the end of the room. White-knuckled grasp, jaw clenched, I scoot my chair as close to the table as I can, then turn to stare at the clock, working the numbers, trying to make things okay, wishing the day hadn't already begun.

Tanya waves her goddamned hand in front of me. "Earth to Jake. Hey, Jake. Aren't you gonna eat?"

The biscuits and gravy have gone cold on my plate; the white sauce has an unnatural sheen to it. I release the table, easing my fingers off the edge.

My chair doesn't slide away.

The clock looks straight now. The room is back in order.

Just. Stop.

Screaming. Surround-sound, high-pitched screams echoing off the walls like we're stuck in an endless corridor.

Kasey shrieks, her voice sharp and piercing.

"I just need some air. Give me a second." I push away from the table, dragging my chair with me, fumbling to set my watch, wind it, get the time back.

I shove my chair in front of the wall clock, covering my

ears from the screams, unable to tell the difference between then and now—what's real and what's in my head.

> *"I'll be right back, Jakey. Look at the time. Here."*
> *She paints a minute and an hour hand on my watch.*
> *"When your black hands line up with these marks, I'll be*
> *here. Take care of Kasey."*

The second hand isn't steady—it catches every time it hits fifty-three seconds, then continues. I hold my watch, my thumb on the face. *One, two, three, flick, one flick, two, flick, three flick* . . . listening for the clicking, whirring sound. Twenty-three times, ninety seconds. Counting. Counting. I shiver, wishing I had a warmer sweatshirt on. *Ten flick, eleven flick, twelve flick* . . .

> *A draft comes from under the door. It's cold. I shiver*
> *and go to the hall closet to pull out my coat. The door swings*
> *and clicks shut behind me, enclosing me in blackness except*
> *for the green light of my Indiglo watch. The doorknob is*
> *jammed.*
> *There's a snap and the sickening sound of bones*
> *breaking—the rat's chest rises and falls, then shudders.*
> *It whines out its last breath, the trap shoved between a*
> *rubbery Halloween clown mask with bulging eyes and*
> *a box of tangled tinsel from last year's Christmas tree.*
> *Silence.*

Somebody rakes her bow across violin strings, *see-saw, see-saw*. Screaming violins.

> *She's awake. "Mama? Mama?" Her voice muffled*
> *by the door.*
> *"She'll be right back!"*
> *"Mama?! Mama?!"*
> *"Stay. Just stay!"*
> *Screaming.*

See-saw, see-saw. Laughing. "*Psycho*, dude. Total *Psycho*. Can you do the banjo duel from *Deliverance?*"

> *I throw myself against the door; it won't open. And*
> *Kasey keeps screaming.*
> *A thud. High-pitched terror.*
> *Muffled sobs.*

The violins stop. The speakers boom: Magic Martin! M&M!

"Speech! Speech! Speech!" They chant.

I swallow back the bubbling acid that works its way up my throat.

> *What if she'd gotten more hurt? What if she'd broken more*
> *than her arm?*
> *What if . . .*
> *Stop it.*

Stop.

I stare at the numbers on the clock, working them out, making the patterns.

A heavy silence until Jenny Roark talks into the microphone. "Apparently, M&M, the greatest athlete to come out of Carson High, is concentrating? On—" She taps my shoulder. "What are you doing?"

"Winding. My. Watch." I try to keep my voice steady. *Tick-tock, tick-tock.*

"Winding his watch," she says.

Luc says, "He's got to be on time one more day. We're all responsible for his punctuality today. Who's going to chaperone Jake to his classes?"

A spray of hands goes up like drowning swimmers— desperate to take on the impossible task of harnessing Jacob Martin's challenged time-management skills.

Everybody cheers.

I push my chair between Mera and Riley, the saxophone guy. "Can I sit here, please? Just for a second?"

Mera nods and dives into a yogurt parfait, like me sitting next to her is the most normal thing in the whole wide world.

Focus. Focus. Focus. I work out the numbers to try to get ahold of the day.

The room has cleared out. I'm still wedged between Mera and Riley. Tanya stands with Luc and Amy at the door—her arms crossed in front of her chest, eyes all red and puffy. Oh Christ.

"Hey, *guevón*!" Luc hollers. "You coming?"

"Thanks," I whisper to Mera, then turn to Riley. "Thanks."

Mera squeezes my arm. "Are you okay, Jake?"

Are you okay?

No. I don't think so.

Wrong answer.

I'd nod if I didn't think my head would explode from excessive movement, so I just grunt, "Uh-huh." Then Luc corrals me into his car and we leave the Nugget, pulling up to Carson High just a few minutes before the bell.

But I've got to get back home—to start the day over.

I have no choice.

FORTY-ONE MERRY-GO-ROUND

Friday, 7:43 a.m.

Seven forty-three. Seven plus four is eleven plus three is fourteen minus seven is seven. OK.

Tanya sniffles all the way to school, pasting a fake smile on her face. She'd probably be a lot less sensitive with a decent meal in her. But I'm smart enough not to say anything. When we get out into the parking lot, Luc pushes me along. "What's wrong with you?" he asks. "Are you *on* something?"

"Yeah. Blackberry protein shakes."

"Don't be an asshole. Be on time. Just today, okay?"

"Sure, Luc, I'm gonna blow the last day of classes off

before the big game. C'mon, man, give me some credit." I sound normal. My voice doesn't even have the slightest hint of panic in it.

"Yeah. Fine." Luc doesn't sound totally convinced. He pulls Amy to his side, squeezing her hand.

Tanya walks off at a distance.

Amy and Luc exchange a glance, but right now I'm too tired to play the game. I can't even muster the strength to ask somebody to give her a fucking Pop-Tart. Or something. Anything with calories.

I need to start the day over.

If I can't do the things in the right order, everything else gets stuck, in that place between the inside and outside door, a limbo-land where nothing ever happens. And tomorrow is too important for me to be stuck, because everything rides on tomorrow. *Everything.*

Luc, Amy, and Tanya's words are lost, floating up to the cold November blue sky, smothered by cartoonlike white clouds. I look up, feeling like I'm in a spinning, snow-globe world, flecks of blue sky being shaken down on top of me. Thoughts, memories, words whirl around my head in chaotic flurries.

Just. Stop. Spinning.

When we were kids, Luc, Mera, and I loved the merry-go-round at Sunset Park. It was one of those rusted ones that have all probably been recalled by now because some kid got tetanus or something just by touching it. Plus it got sizzling hot—third-degree-burn hot—in the middle of summer. It was wobbly, and when we ran to push it, on one side we'd almost blow out a knee because of the funky angle. But then we'd all jump on and lie down, letting the sky spin above us. It was a horrible, good sick feeling being dizzy like that, flat on our backs, feeling like the world was spinning out of control, and the only place that we were safe was on the merry-go-round.

But it was stuck—stuck turning around and around on the same axle in the same place. We never actually went anywhere, so when we got off, it was like "Fuck. That's it?"

Then we'd do it again because we really believed that one day the spinning would take us where we wanted to go.

I'm still spinning; I'm still stuck.

Today, I need to start over, so I can get to tomorrow and leave the webs and spiders and the *tick-tock* behind. Tomorrow is my day.

Mental inventory of time available to go home, touch flamingo, get inside, get back in bed, get up, shower, touch grandfather clock. Thirty-five minutes. Lunch. That's not a problem. I just have to make it through the first two blocks and get a car.

There's gotta be at least five to six hundred kids in each

grade, a third of whom might drive to school, so that leaves me with a possible seven hundred cars that I can use. I only know one guy who *might* let me use his.

Fuck.

Maybe I should've worked on maintenance Kasey style over the past four years and developed an ongoing relationship with somebody, besides Luc, with a car.

In first-period government class, Ms. Baker pairs us up and tells us we have to brainstorm a list of possible senior project ideas to hand in to her by the end of the period. Everything in my body has frozen, replaying the order of the morning, ticking off all the things I left undone.

Tick-tock, tick-tock.

I can hear the scratch of each pencil, the rub of erasers and swipe of red rubber shavings on the floor. The sounds meld together like the heavy drone of eardrum-blowing cicadas with flicking wings and buckling tymbals. I tap my ears and look around.

Nobody else hears the buzz.

It's like watching a bunch of domesticated turkeys drowning in the rain because they don't close their fucking beaks. They're all *suffocating.*

They can't know that everything is wrong because things only work when I start the day right. Today can't happen until I start again.

What if . . .

They keep gobbling, scribbling, totally fucking oblivious. They all act like it's okay.

It's not okay.

I have to start over.

I can't leave home before dawn—before the routine—because if I do . . . I don't know how to finish that sentence.

What if we lose tomorrow?

What if Kasey gets hurt because I didn't touch the grandfather clock?

What if Mom really hits a cyclist or Dad gets in a car accident at work?

We. Can't. Lose. Tomorrow. Everything I am is riding on tomorrow.

Ms. Baker circulates the room like a predatory hawk; her talons—age-spotted fingers with nicotine-stained nails, ridged and thick—swipe across the desks to look at what people write.

I count, tapping the face of my watch, playing with the numbers raining through gaping holes in my brain.

8:08

Eight-oh-eight. Eight plus eight is sixteen. Eight minus eight is zero. Eight divided by eight is one.

Fuck.

Eight times eight is sixty-four minus eight is fifty-six divided by . . . Fuck.

I can't get the numbers to work either.

It's so fucking loud.

"Jacob, what are you going to do your senior project on?" she says. The sound of her words blends together with the scratch of pencils and rub of erasers until I hear a deafening buzz.

I write "cicadas" on my sheet of paper.

"Bugs?" she says. "You're going to do your senior government project on bugs?"

"Bugs," I say. "Cicadas—the Magicicada."

"Keep your voice down, Jacob. I can hear just fine."

But how can she hear above the hum—the batting wings and popping tymbals?

"Would you like to tell me why? As your advisor, I need something more concrete than a bug's name to approve the project."

"The noise," I say, leaning my head on the desk.

"You don't need to whisper, Mr. Martin. I don't appreciate the attitude." Ms. Baker takes my paper. "You want bugs, you got bugs."

I can tell she thinks she's going to teach me a lesson. Ms. Baker wanders around the room, deaf to the wing-flicking drone. I can't get rid of the noise.

I write one to five hundred on my paper and go through the algorithm.

When I finish the chart, the primes pop out at me in three dimensions. They float off the page and circle my head like a swarm of bumblebees. When I reach out for them, everything goes back to its two-dimensional reality. But looking close, I can see the bulge of the numbers on the page, how they swell and are ready to float away again.

I mentally check off the things I'll need to do in the thirty-five-minute lunch break. Because if I don't do them . . .

Tick-tock.

I just need to start the day over.

FORTY-THREE STUCK

Friday, 9:37 a.m.

Nine thirty-seven. Nine plus three is twelve plus seven is nineteen.
OK.

During nutrition I find Luc. "Luc, man. You've gotta lend me your car. I've got a killer headache and need Advil or something. I'll pick it up during lunch."

Luc shoves his keys into his pocket. "Go to the nurse."

"C'mon, she can't give me anything but a Band-Aid."

"You can't take anything anyway. Tomorrow's the big game. Scouts mean peeing in cups. So suck it up and have a glass of water."

"Luc, I *need* something." My palms itch from touching

the flamingo this morning and not going back in. I stare down and see the first signs of blisters—pink welts forming. I shove my hands into Luc's face. "See. I just need to get home to get things taken care of."

Luc pushes my hands down. "What are you talking about?"

I look down. My palms burn, but the welts are gone. I run my fingers across the tender skin. Nothing.

I'm fucking crazy.

Crazy.

"Can you lend me the Dart or not?" The probability that he might actually say yes is about as great as me having a sexual encounter that doesn't include *Manuela.*

"No fucking way. You're not going to do this to us. If you're late, we're screwed. Today, it's not just about *you*, it's about the team. And it's about somebody here doing *something*."

"Don't say there's no *I* in team," I say, trying to make a joke, keeping my voice steady. "Luc, I've got thirty-five minutes. I just need to get some shit cleared up at home." My palms still burn, but when I look down, the only things I see are the half-moon indentations of my nails.

"Deal with your weird shit on your own time. *Guevón, lo que estás haciendo es una chimbada.*" And he goes off in Spanish. Luc turns into channel seventy-three, Univision, when he's pissed.

I don't even need the translation to know he's ready to kill me.

Kids stare at us and move away. We're officially making a scene.

Mighty Luc. Moses. Parting the sea of blue in Carson High's hallways. I had counted on him giving me the keys. He doesn't get it.

How could he?

He's a suffocating turkey.

I push past him down the hall, and he grabs at my shirt collar. "Goddamnit, Martin. What's your fucking problem?"

I shrug him off. "I'm fine. Just forget about it." I hear myself speak the words in a normal, unwavering voice. But my pulse thrums against my temples and I can hardly breathe. I need to get my hands under a stream of icy water, and I push to the front of the drinking-fountain line.

9:42

Nine forty-two. Nine plus four is thirteen minus two is eleven. OK.

Some kid says, "Dude, I hope you washed your hands."

"That's what I'm doing now." My voice sounds like I'm one violin pluck away from going major *twang*. "I burned myself. That's all."

Keep it cool.

Things get blotchy, so I splash my face with the metallic water that tastes like ice-cold liquid public-bathroom

123

paper-towel dispenser. I swallow and splash, swallow and splash.

Kids move away.

When I stand up, Luc's right behind me. He scowls, his caterpillar eyebrows touching. I wait to see if they'll crawl off his face. "I'll get you an Advil or something at lunch," he says.

9:45

Nine forty-five. Nine plus four is thirteen plus five is eighteen divided by nine is two. OK.

The bell rings. "At lunch," I echo. "Can't be late." I head to science, pushing back the webs and *buzz, buzz, buzz* in between my ears.

Mrs. Hayes has set up one of her forensic labs: death and decomposition. When we walk into class, it's filled with jars of things we're supposed to smell. We're supposed to walk around describing the scents; the last station involves dissecting a fetal pig.

> *The rat's chest moves up and down, up and down until it shudders and the rat stops moving, its abdomen pinched in the trap.*

I push the memory away and focus on the blue smudge in the upper right-hand corner of the whiteboard. Mrs. Hayes has that excited-to-impart-knowledge look in her eyes. She's one of those "forward-thinking" teachers. But sometimes it's just gross.

Mariana Ramirez gets all fainty when she walks into class, and Dawn Washington takes her to the library. They're doing the work sheet option for this lab. Mera flat-out refuses to do it, saying that it's wrong to use animals this way, and she snatches another work sheet out of Mrs. Hayes's hands and gathers things at her desk.

I'm paired with Seth, class president and all-around prick, if you ask me. If you stuck pencil lead up his ass, he'd pop out diamonds. I steady the trembling in my hands, but all I can do is think about getting home.

And not puking in science. Sometimes I wish I could be a chick and get all fainty.

"If anybody else wants to go to the library, raise your hand," Mrs. Hayes says, kind of last minute, her white lab coat speckled with unknown brown stuff.

My hand shoots up. Death. I already know what it smells like.

Diaz kicks me from behind and says, "Good thing you've got a dick on the field." He and Simpson crack up. Darius Simpson—the eternal bench warmer for the team. His ass is one giant splinter.

Diaz says something else that I don't quite hear—something about penis size and lack of pubic hair.

Mrs. Hayes hands me a work sheet and hall pass. Mera

walks in front of me. I inhale the stale smell of the hallway—sweat socks, BO, curdled milk, normal. Not decomposed bodies. I hurry my pace to walk with Mera to the library.

"I couldn't do that lab," I finally say when I know that opening my mouth won't lead to projectile vomiting.

"Last period," says Mera, "three kids went to the nurse throwing up. Personally, I think it's pretty crappy to use a pig like that. It's just wrong. I'm going to start a letter-writing campaign to Congress in protest so that we stop using animals in high-school labs."

Mera's going all PETA now, ranting about animal rights and how if whales and elephants are vegetarians—the biggest mammals on earth—why couldn't we be? Her face gets red splotches when she's mad—making her wispy blond hair look almost transparent, like a halo.

"Mrs. Hayes is definitely gonna have a bunch of parent phone calls tonight," I say when Mera takes a breath. Last time Mrs. Hayes did a "lifelike" lab, it was on evidence collection. She hired some actor to play dead. He looked dead. Real dead—blue lips, stiff, some kid even said he felt waxy. Not likely—I mean the waxy-skin thing. Anyway, someone ended up calling the police because they thought Mrs. Hayes had whacked a guy for the sake of education.

I laugh. A little. The burning in my skull has moved to my gut. The knot in my stomach just gets tighter and tighter until it feels like my colon is going to turn inside out. We sit together at a table—across from Dawn and Mariana. The words in the encyclopedia on decomposition blur together. I stare at the clock. Time ticks away.

Mera's pencil scratches on her work sheet; Dawn and Mariana are way ahead, working together. I scoot toward Mera.

"Mera," I whisper, "I need to borrow your car."

"What for?"

"I've gotta go home at lunch. I'll be back for last block. Please," I say.

"Have lunch at the cafeteria like normal kids."

"I need to go home," I say, resting my head on the cool library table that faintly smells like window cleaner.

Mera's eyebrows arch. "No. Get over yourself, Jake. I'm not indebted to you because we talked for two minutes yesterday. You have fifteen soccer buddies—all with nice cars. Ask one of them."

My world is reduced to Luc. That's all I have. Kase doesn't count because she can't drive. Luc. That's it. Pretty small fucking world. "I can't," I say. "I can't ask them."

"*Shhhh.*" Mariana looks up from her work sheet. "*Some people* are trying to work."

Mera flips her off. How to win friends and influence people—Mera style.

I swallow a laugh. "You never change."

"How would you know?" she asks. "It's not like

we've been in touch."

I tap my pencil on the table and mutter, "I guess I've known you since I was old enough to know things."

Mera smiles.

"So?" I say.

"Why?"

"Because I need to start the day over."

Mera stares at me with her mannequin eyes. But this time I don't look away.

She hands the keys to me. "But you better fill up the tank."

"What?" I say. "Christ, I'm only going home and back."

"Well, everything has a price now, doesn't it?"

"Goddamnit," I mutter. I already owe Luc for last night's coffee run plus "interest," as he puts it. I shove the keys in my pocket, then turn to the clock, working out the numbers. Before the bell rings, the four of us walk back to class, my work sheet conspicuously blank.

Mrs. Hayes looks up and says, "What's with this? What did you do for ninety minutes?"

"I was—" I don't figure telling her that working out prime numbers from the time would be an acceptable answer. "It's just, I'm stuck."

"Stuck?"

I nod. It's the most honest thing I've said in the past five years. "I'm stuck." It's the only thing that explains why I do what I do.

Mera interrupts. "We worked together. He jammed his finger at soccer practice."

Mariana huffs behind us and Mera shoots her a look: one head-swivel, kryptonite–projectile vomit away from demonic possession. Major intimidation.

The bell rings, and I run, leaving Mera behind with Mrs. Hayes and my blank work sheet. I zigzag through the cafeteria out into the parking lot, avoiding Luc and the other guys. Mera's van isn't hard to find. She's probably the only chick at school who drives a van. And that, for many guys I know, is a major waste of horizontal space.

The van reeks of patchouli in a lame attempt to cover years of raw meat. I rev the engine and tear out of the parking lot, flying over the speed bumps. The lot gates close ten minutes after lunch bell. I honk and try to butt into the line of cars.

I turn on the radio. *Classical music? C'mon, Mera, you're killing me.* I flick it to K-Play AM sports and turn the volume to nothing, then crank it up thirteen notches. In five minutes I'll be home. Less than five minutes.

My phone rings. After three rings, I turn it off. "Fuck them. I've got time," I mutter.

I just need to start the day over. It's not that big a deal. I know that this isn't right. It's not normal. But it's what I do.

Because I need the magic.

FORTY-SEVEN GENESIS

Friday, 11:43 a.m.

Eleven forty-three. One plus one is two plus four is six plus three is nine minus four is five. OK.

I don't rub the flamingo beak; I already did this morning, so I rush up the front steps, into the house and my room, setting the clock, undressing, and jumping into bed.

And everything's going to be fine. I close my eyes and turn on my side to face the clock. Ready to begin the day.

I open my left eye, count to three, then open my right eye.

One plus one is two plus seven is nine minus four is five. OK.

Eleven forty-seven and fifty-five.

I slip my left foot out from under the covers and count.
One, two, three.

Fifty-six, fifty-seven—

Right foot. *One, two, three.*

Fifty-eight, fifty-nine.

Up.

My shoulders relax as the tension drains from my body.
I can hear the phone ringing, but I block out the noise. The
machine will pick it up. Plus it's too early for phone calls. It's
Genesis. The beginning. He had to do it right. Begin with
the heavens and the earth.

I have to do it right.

I have to begin my day.

Ring. Ring.

Just ignore the phone. I walk to the bathroom. Damp
towels are thrown over the half-closed curtain—starting to
smell like mildew. I do a quick cleanup, organize the towels
and shampoo bottles just right, and jump into the shower,
forty-seven seconds on each side, and out and dressed and
rushing downstairs.

*Just have to make it through the routine. Go through the
steps.*

I shake off the bad feeling that I'm doing everything too
abbreviated. Half-assed. That it'll just be some hack way to
get back the magic I lost this morning. *Tomorrow, I think.
Tomorrow I can do everything double.*

I tap the grandfather clock three times, opening the door with both hands. The door closes behind me with a click. I look at my watch.

11:54

Eleven fifty-four. One plus one is two plus five is seven plus four is eleven. OK.

I turn and see Mom standing in the driveway, staring at the car's bumper. I didn't even hear her drive up.

Not now, I think. *Not today. I can't do it today.* I walk toward Mera's van, keys jangling in my hand, when Mom calls out to me. "Jake!"

"Hey, Mom." I wave at her.

"Oh Jake! Oh my God, Jake. I think—" She covers her face with shaking hands. "I hit a cyclist. I tried to avoid him. I really did. But I know I hit him. Oh God, Jake. Oh my God." She stares at the bumper, then drops to her hands and knees, going over every inch of it with a magnifying glass.

"Mom." I walk over to her. "Mom, what are you doing?"

"Blood. Looking for blood. Oh God, Jake."

"Stand up, Mom." I pull her up off her knees and cradle her head on my shoulder. "See, Mom? There's no blood here. Or dents. Or anything." I try to reason with her. "If you had hit a cyclist, there'd be dents. Something, *anything* to show for it. There's nothing here."

The numbers of the clock in my head whir. Time has

sped up now, just to fuck with me. Just to make sure I'll be late. *Fuck, fuck, fuck.*

I've got to be on time.

Tomorrow I've got to play because all of this has to end.

"We've got to go. Go back and make sure," she pleads. She whispers, "I was real tired this morning. So tired. But then I had to get the groceries. I didn't think—"

I look in the car and see the ice cream carton's edges have softened; pink drips down the side and puddles on the passenger seat. Dad's going to shit.

"Get in the van," I say. "We'll drive by where you passed the cyclist; then I'll leave you to get a cab." I pull out my empty wallet. "You have cash?"

But she's back on her hands and knees, staring at the bumper, scraping some bird shit off the chipped chrome. I pull her back up. "C'mon. Don't do that," I say, and usher her to Mera's van, helping her into the passenger side.

I pull away from the house and head toward Safeway.

"No," Mom says. "Costco."

"Costco? Since when do you shop at Costco?"

"I just thought. It'd be easier there. No bicycle paths. But look what I've done." Her hand shakes as she dials her cell phone. "Yes. I'm just wondering if there's been a hit-and-run reported off Old Clear Creek Road. Yes. Yes, sir. I'll hold."

I snatch the phone from her and hang up. "Jesus Christ,

Mom. Don't do that. Don't call the cops. You know you can't call them about that stuff anymore."

I take the back roads until we have to turn onto Highway 395. How the hell am I going to explain this to Coach, Luc, the principal? Dad? I look at Mom. She rubs her hands together, wrapping her fingers around her knuckles—rubbing, wrapping, gazing absently out the window.

It's just a game. A game with twenty-two guys running around a field after a ball. Why does it have to be everything?

I cup my hand over hers.

She wipes a tear from her cheek and swallows as I turn up Old Clear Creek Road, eyes scanning the road for signs of death.

We drive to Costco, through the parking lot, and down the road again. We stop where Mom saw the cyclist, and we get out of the car looking for signs of any kind of accident. "See? Nothing."

She exhales. "Nothing."

I won't look at the time now. I can't. It's too late. Everything was wrong from the beginning today anyway.

Mom wraps her frail arms around me. "Thank you, Jake. Thank you."

"It's nothing. C'mon. I'll take you home."

"You'll be late," she says in a lame attempt at being a mom.

"I won't be late."

She accepts this as the truth because she needs to get home fast and go to bed. Maybe drink something. I don't know.

I mentally organize the afternoon. It's like trying to piece together the remains of an explosion, putting together the puzzle of shards so it'll look like the day it was supposed to be.

What if I can't play tomorrow? What if the spiders never leave?

I swallow down the possibility. There's gotta be a way to play—to get to class—to make it up. I'll fucking do detention for the rest of the year.

I just need tomorrow. I need the game.

When we pull into the driveway, Dad's car is parked behind Mom's. He's walking melted groceries into the house; his uniform is sticky from the ice cream and who knows what else. He turns and sees Mom and me in the van and nods.

Mom wrings her hands. "We can't tell him."

"We won't."

"Thank you, Jake," she says, and steps out of the van. "Have a good day at school," she says. She walks toward the house, wisps of dandelion hair blowing in the wind. I rev the van up and drive away before Dad comes out of the house.

* * *

1:23 p.m.

One twenty-three. Good number. One plus two is three plus three is six divided by two is three. OK. One times two is two plus three is five. OK.

I wonder since I missed a class if that's technically being late.

FIFTY-THREE MERA'S SONG

Friday, 1:31 p.m.

One thirty-one. One plus three is four plus one is five. OK.

I pull into Mera's parking spot and work my way to the side of the building. Some ROTC kids are walking in, and I slip in the doors behind them.

Perfect record.

I walk down the empty hallways. It's already last block. It's pretty stupid to be here at all. I should've just stayed in Mera's van until it was time to dress out for practice, but there's something great about wandering around empty school halls, not having to avoid anybody, not having to hide.

I peek into a classroom where some substitute is trying to break up a fight. I wander past the drama theater and band room. The horn section of the band is working on a new song—something for the winter concert. I pause. It sounds like "Winter Wonderland." Kind of.

I work my way to the auditorium. It's dark except for a dim stage light. Mera's sitting, drawing her bow across the strings. I slip in the door and sit in the shadows, leaning my head back against the chair, listening to the repetitive song, how she plays it louder and louder, the same notes, the same melody.

In the background there's a CD playing a rhythm—on a drum. The longer Mera plays, the more it feels like the notes she's playing are trying to break free of the steady background beat. A couple of times it's almost like she'll make it, like the notes will change, but then she pauses a few beats and begins again.

The beat doesn't change. Her notes don't change, and no matter how hard she saws on that violin, she's stuck in the same melody.

Then there's this weird, discordant note and a fitful end. It's over.

The ending leaves me unsettled. As if the melody gave in to the tapping of the drum, the rattle of nails rapping a window.

Mera sits on the stage, her chin resting on the violin,

the CD whirring to a stop, then looks up where I'm sitting, shading her eyes with the palm of her hand. "Fine. Church songs and people. Sperm donor: 'My Cup Runneth Over.'"

"Sperm clinic nurse: 'Kumbaya.'" I pronounce it "Cum-Boy-Yeah."

She cracks up. "That's cheating."

"Somebody in this country, somewhere, would pronounce it like that."

"Fair enough."

I laugh and feel the tension ease out of my shoulders. Mera covers her eyes from the glare of the overhead stage light and looks my direction. "Why are you always hiding?"

"I'm not hiding."

"Whatever, Magic Martin."

I rub my sticky palms on my sweatpants. "You hide too," I finally say.

She looks up to where I'm sitting.

"You do. Behind your anger and I-don't-give-a-shit attitude. Because you *do* give a shit. We all hide. We're not so different."

"You know what your problem is?" Her voice is tight.

I don't. But I sure would like somebody to tell me. We stare at each other across the dark auditorium.

Mera stands up and moves the music stand across the stage in a horrific screech. She unplugs the CD player and cradles it under her arm, holding her violin with the other hand. She shakes her head and sighs. "Never mind. Anyway, it's *Bolero*. By Ravel."

"*Bolero*," I echo.

"They say he had frontotemporal dementia when he wrote it, which might explain the fact he wrote a sixteen-minute, one-movement song." When she talks, her words echo off the auditorium walls, so even though she's standing in front of me, it sounds like she's coming from everywhere.

"Frontotemporal dementia?" I ask.

"Yeah. His brain was getting all mushy." She stands, staring at the darkness, then starts flapping her arms up and down. "'You *dare* to come to me for a heart, do you? You clinking, clanking, clattering collection of caliginous junk!'"

I stifle a laugh. It's nice to know somebody's as weird as me in this world.

"'Pay no attention to that man behind the curtain!'" She puts her hands on her hips. "Okay, Oz, time to come out."

I stay seated, wishing she'd just keep playing.

"Weird-o." She whistles and leaves the stage just as the bell rings.

But the music's still here, in the air, the beat still pounding in my head, keeping the melody trapped inside those short, even notes. I listen until a crackly voice interrupts the drumming: "*Jacob Martin*."

Oh fuck. I'm totally losing it. Totally.

The voice repeats: *"Jacob Martin."* This time clearer.

And I wonder if crazy people think they can hear God. Or what if I *do* hear God? And it's a chick. Like who's gonna believe that?

It sounds like thunder followed by heavy breathing: *"Jacob Martin, please report to the attendance office."*

I shake my head and look up. The school intercom is right above me.

I leave the auditorium, running into half the orchestra. "Hey, man, they're looking for you," some kid says.

"Yeah. Thanks," I say, pretty relieved I'm not hearing voices, too.

Yet.

Maybe I have that brain-mush problem.

"Hey. Good luck on Saturday!" He waves at me. Friendly. Nice. "You're totally wick."

"Did you just say *wick*?" some other kid asks.

"Well, yeah. Wick. You know. As in wicked. But short."

"Not as in candle?"

"C'mon, Craig, you can't tell me you've never heard *wick* before?"

And I'm out of earshot before the orchestra determines whether *wick* is an appropriate abbreviation for *wicked*, which would mean I'm pretty much amazing.

Which I'm not.

FIFTY-NINE REVIVING THE DEAD

Friday, 2:03 p.m.

Two-oh-three. Two plus three is five. OK.

I dress out in Mera's van and watch everybody stream out of the school. When I squint, it looks like everybody's drowning, heads bobbing up and down in a sea of Carson High blue. And there are no lifeboats.

I turn my phone on. Seventeen missed calls from Luc. One from Kase.

Kase. I'll talk to her tonight. She can tell me about her day. And everything will go back the way it needs to be.

Nobody says anything when I walk out onto the field. Luc's seething. Major Univision mode.

Fuck you, I want to say. *Fuck you fuck you fuck you fuck you.*

And the closet smells return—damp boots, last year's wool sweaters, forgotten half-eaten sandwiches in coat pockets—all faintly masking the musty animal smell—that sterilized sick-dog veterinarian-clinic smell.

The whisper of death.

If I could just go back to the day before *that night and do things right, change the order, I wouldn't be like this.*

The spiders stop spinning on the loom of my brain. That night, stuck in the closet, waiting for the time on my Indiglo to match Mom's squiggly clock hand, they came to stay. I'd felt the spiders before, but after that night . . . That's when I figured out how to keep them back—how to count them away.

It's like all this time they've been waiting for perfection.

Tomorrow is perfection. Tomorrow I will be normal.

I catch myself and reverse my thoughts.

There's nothing wrong with how I am. Nothing.

Fuck you.

The team sits in a circle, stretching to Luc's count. I strap on my guards and start to warm up, running around the field. I don't need them.

They need me.

They need the magic.

So when I make the goals, everything will be okay. Life will go back to normal. We'll win the game and it'll all be over. The spiders will disappear.

Then I can just walk away.

Coach is talking to Principal Vaughn. A bright blue vein throbs in Vaughn's temple—a neon strip against his blotchy, sun-damaged forehead. Vaughn's suit jacket and pants flap in the wind. The only thing not moving is his gelled hair.

The wind has wrapped his purple tie around his neck, and he yanks on it, trying to keep it from sailing behind him.

I put my head down and run.

Coach hollers at Luc. "Get the nets out for soccer tennis, Luc! You've stretched enough." His hands are balled in fists at his sides, his face a scrunched raisin.

Luc catches up to me and says, "*Hijo de puta*. You're total smegma. Just one fucking day to be on time. One day to normal out."

"Fuck you," I say under my breath. *I am normal.*

Then all I feel is the pounding. Luc becomes his dad— his clenched fists and hate words. The sour smell of his breath and bloodshot eyes.

I try to push the thoughts away—to stay away from that night—but I can't breathe with Luc lying on my chest.

Her screams have stopped. I don't know what's worse,
the screaming or the way the house creaks in the wind,
the tick-tock of the grandfather clock with its heavy

*pendulum swinging back and forth, pushing through the
thick silence of the house.*

"Kasey! Kasey, answer me!"

*I stand up, pushing myself off the ground, my hand
grazing the thick rat tail. I jump back, knocking over a
box of Halloween decorations, shiny plastic clown masks,
glow-in-the-dark skulls.*

What if she's hurt? Or worse?

*My heart pounds and pumps blood through my body.
I kick against the door with the heels of my feet, then
crumple to the floor, pushing in the Indiglo light to see the
time, concentrate on the numbers.*

*Working the numbers in the fluorescent green light is
the only thing to keep the spiders from eating me alive—
the only thing to keep Kasey safe out there.*

"Fight back, *marica*." Luc pounds and pounds.

What if . . .

"This game is everything. And you're gonna fucking
blow it."

The thoughts whirl around my head—some kind of car-
nival *Wheel of Fortune* with all the *what if*s gyrating, waiting
for the wheel to stop when it slows down to its final *tick,
tick, tick.*

I search for my watch, to see the time.

But I can't move—pinned under Luc.

I feel panic rise inside me like a crashing wave. Terror. My heart pounds harder and faster—a jackhammer against my body. A scream gets trapped in my mind and shatters into thousands of pieces.

What if . . .

The pounding, the hate, the anger go on until Diaz grabs Luc and holds him back. Luc spits a long, spiraling blood loogie that explodes into thousands of minibubbles in the air, all spattering my left leg.

I lie on the prickly grass and curl my legs to my chest, closing my eyes, waiting for the earth to swallow me up. *Two, three, five, seven, eleven . . . one hundred three . . . two hundred seventy-seven. . . .*

I look at the distorted faces through the slit that was once my right eye and feel the Pop Rocks blood vessels exploding under my skin, spilling into my tissues all over my chest, face, neck, and back. *Pop. Pop. Pop.*

Coach and Principal Vaughn drag us into the main office. Coach leaves Diaz to run practice, saying, "Nobody leaves. Nobody. Until we get this sorted out."

I inhale. When I breathe in, there's a sharp pain in my chest. I think about Kase. Maybe I'll get my one phone call. I can call her right now. Maybe that would make things better. It would just be better to talk to someone.

Anyone.

I turn to Luc. He's gone, turned into his dad, so I look

away. All the *what if*s crowd my brain—pushing aside anything else. The only thing that helps are the numbers and the routines—getting things back on track.

This whole week has been fucked, like parts of me are leaking all over the place—parts that nobody should know about. And now they do because there's no way to make things right. Fix them. They went wrong, way wrong, too long ago.

So maybe I have to tell them about the numbers and Mom's imaginary bicyclist. Maybe I have to tell them about why I had to go home and why I had to stay at home. Why I had to start over. Why I had to help Mom.

Maybe I won't have to hide it anymore.

Maybe that's okay, too.

I press the ice pack the school nurse, Mrs. Quincy, gives me against my eye.

After a while, soft footsteps pad down the hallway and Dad shows up. He's changed out of his UPS uniform into jeans and a polo. I guess he must've stayed home with Mom this afternoon after all. He pats my shoulder and sits next to me. "Hi, Luc," he says.

Luc nods at him and looks down at his shoes.

We listen to the muffled voices coming from Principal Vaughn's office. Rumbles and growls punctuated by thumping fists on desks. I close my eyes and count.

Luc's mom's heels make a *clackity-clack* sound on the

tile floor. She always smells like vanilla and car grease. She owns Jumpstart Mechanics on Highway 50. I sometimes wish she was my mom—the kind who gives bear hugs and bakes fresh banana bread. But she's got a biblical temper. Old Testament.

One time Luc let Juancho, his older brother, duct tape him to the floor. Mrs. Camacho came in and saw Luc red-faced, struggling to get loose while Juancho held me back. She said something to the effect of "If you're stupid enough to let your brother duct tape you to the kitchen floor, you can stay there all night," followed by a string of colorful words you only hear at Boca Juniors soccer games. Then she sent me home.

Mrs. Camacho ruffles my hair. "Hello, Ha-co-bo." She always pronounces my name in Spanish, and it sounds kind of like she's going to hock a loogie when she does. But I like it.

"Hi, Mrs. Camacho."

Then she yanks Luc by the ear and says, *"Culicagado, ¿usted en qué estaba pensando? ¿Usted va a ser igualito a su papá? ¿o qué?"* She starts soft; then her voice rises into a crescendo, masking the sounds coming from Principal Vaughn and Coach. The entire room fills with words until the walls look like they're going to crack under pressure. The only thing stopping them is Dad's silence, sucking the words back in.

I wish Dad would yell like that.

Just throw the fucking punch.

Instead he treats everything with long-drawn-out silences, punctuated by catch-all phrases: *Don't disappoint us. This is your future. This is your responsibility.* It's like life has been a giant disappointment to him and I'm an extension of that disappointment.

Finally Coach and Principal Vaughn come out of Vaughn's office. I see sweat beading on Coach's forehead, and he swipes it away with his shirt sleeve. Vaughn has rings under his pits larger than Saturn's.

It's time to come clean. I swallow and fight back the burning in my eyes and nose—the stinging tears that threaten to slip down my cheeks.

Just as I'm about to talk, Dad stands up. "He was at home with his mother. She's not well. She called him so he could be with her until I showed up. I just couldn't miss a whole day of work."

My truth is swallowed up by his—or the one he and Mom made up this afternoon. Reality. Perception. Truth. Lies. The lines are blurred.

Vaughn deflates in front of us, the air swooshing out of his thin frame until he looks like a wet paper doll ready to double over. Even his gelled hair has lost its sheen. I guess I won't be the example he needs to set for his tough new tardy policy.

Dad rubs his hands on his jeans and says, "She's

sometimes not well." Every word is like pulling razor blades out of his throat.

Not well? Mom's a fucking nutcase. She left us the day she left a seven-year-old to take care of his four-year-old sister because she had to retrace her steps from the past four days to make sure she hadn't killed anybody.

Mom's not "not well."

Mom's gone.

How come he doesn't say that? How come he doesn't *tell the truth*?

"He won't be late again. I'll make sure of it," Dad says.

"And the fight . . . ," Vaughn says. But he's on shaky ground now. What happens at soccer is Coach's jurisdiction. Coach's call.

"What fight?" Coach asks.

Vaughn and Coach start arguing again.

Luc mutters, "Why didn't you tell me it was about your mom, asshole, instead of the Advil shit?"

I shrug.

"Sorry."

"'S okay," I say. I think my lip is a little swollen, too.

He elbows me and grins. We get away with it again. This time, maybe just for once, I don't feel like hiding anymore. But I wouldn't know where to begin—how to explain it to anybody because it sounds too crazy. I sound too crazy.

My head pounds. I turn to Dad. "Did you get Kase?" I

ask under my breath.

He nods. "She's with Mom."

Yeah. The ghost.

Dad clears his throat and says, "Thank you, Jacob."

Vaughn and Coach have come to some kind of agreement about Luc and me attending a feel-good workshop: *Love Yourself, Embrace the Anger.*

Dad and Mrs. Camacho leave. I try to ignore the slouch in Dad's shoulders. He'll get home to Kase. That's all that matters now. But something still itches at the back of my mind—the spiders are released, so I slip back to the numbers—the comfort—and count how many times each person speaks in the room until we're set free and can go back to soccer practice.

SIXTY-ONE CONFESSION

Friday, 5:12 p.m.

Five twelve. Five plus one is six plus two is eight minus five is three. OK.

Coach takes out his cache of team-building crap and dumps it on the field. He consults his book and decides we should do "minefield," starting with Luc and me. I'm blindfolded and Luc has to guide me around a bunch of obstacles by giving me spoken directions.

Luc's a decent guide. I get through most of the stuff until I land on my ass in a bucket of icy water. When I take off the blindfold, the team cheers. Luc says, "*Guevón.*"

We're okay, a team again. I'll get to go home and just zone out.

But Coach isn't done with us yet. We move into the school gym. Mats are spread around it. We do trust-fall shit. And when we're done, we sit back to back. Coach says, "Now it's confession time."

There's a collective groan.

But I think part of us kind of likes this—being forced to *say* something.

"You know the drill. Like/Dislike/Like. Be real. Let's go."

Luc and I lean against each other. "You first," he says.

"Okay. Like." I take a breath. "I like that you wait for me in the morning, even when I'm having a tough time getting out of the house."

Luc pauses. "Like. I like your honey-colored eyes." And he cracks up. I hate that. I hate that everything has to be a joke to him.

I start to stand up and he yanks me back down. "Okay. Okay. Like." He lowers his voice. "I like that you haven't told anybody that I do that choir shit for church. And, *guevón*, if anybody ever finds out I vote for contestants on *American Idol*, I'll kick your ass to next week."

Silence.

This is the first time Luc has ever said anything real to me. It's as if he actually wants to talk today. The preconceptions slip away.

We're just us, whoever that is.

We sit in silence. The rules are we don't comment. We

just listen and let whatever's been said be said.

"Fuck, man, are you gonna go or what?" Some of the players are already done, sitting around the free-throw circle where we'll end this. But part of me wants to let it sink in and just be here.

Be real, not who Luc wants to see.

"Okay. Dislike." I try to find a way to say it even though I think my brain's wiring has shorted. "I dislike those times when you become your dad. Like this afternoon. Because—" *Because it reminds me of all the times I was never a real friend.* My voice drifts off.

I sigh.

All the shit I carry with me—the time, the magic— floats away for a second, leaving me lighter. Free.

I hold on to that little bit of truth until I feel Luc tense up—his back knots and his words come out like venom. "Dislike. I dislike that you're a total *marica*. You didn't see me pissing myself every time he hit me, because every time he hit me was one fewer time he'd hit my mom. It started when I was five and ended the night he got blitzed and crashed his car. Seven years. Fists. Belts. One time a chain. I am not my dad—"

If you're not bleeding, you're not hurt.

I realize what's real is what he just said; my made-up numbers world doesn't matter. What happened in the closet, waiting for Mom to come home, doesn't matter.

How could that matter?

What's real is that everything I feel isn't.

And it's too late to ask him if he's okay. I should've asked him when we were five, when I saw the first bruises. A simple question. *Luc, are you okay?*

"Your turn," he says, his voice a low hiss.

"Like," I say. "I like that—" I swallow back the lump that has formed in my throat, pushing down my words, sifting through the avalanche of thoughts until I pick the right one—the one Luc will approve of. "Like," I whisper. "I like that tomorrow we'll win our third state championship in a row."

The tension flows out of Luc's back and voice when he says, "Like. I like that we'll win our third state championship in a row and we'll be heroes. It's our time."

I can hear the pride in his voice. This is it for Luc. At the end of the year, he'll go work at his mom's mechanic shop. He doesn't care about college. That's what he says. That's what his mom says. "Your duty is to your family."

It seems to me he's already paid his dues.

All our lives Luc and I have been in that place between the inside and outside door—navigating no-man's land— just trying to get through the day.

Luc grabs my hand and yanks me up. "Dude, man, this is our time. We can't fuck it up."

Meaning, *You can't fuck it up.*

"Yeah," I say, feeling drained, and wonder if it's possible to sweep up broken illusions and glue them back together.

We gather in a circle with the team. Coach's voice is gravelly and hoarse. Principal Vaughn really takes it out of him. Coach squeezes each of us on the shoulder and says, "Now, we're way past big-speech time. I want to thank you for the last few months. It's been very special for me. Anybody have anything to say?"

Diaz leans over and says, "*Hoosiers.*"

Coach doesn't have scriptwriters, not like Hollywood. So why not use the movie stuff?

"'And David put his hand in the bag and took out a stone and slung it. And struck the Philistine on the head. And he fell to the ground.'" Coach exhales. "Amen."

We're quiet.

"Coach, man, aren't *we* Goliath this time around?" Keller asks. Leave it to Keller to get all specific about it.

Coach stumbles over his words. "Well, Keller, I never thought about it that way." Coach isn't a dumb man. He's just quiet. And good at what he does. He fights for us, and when I play, part of it is just for him. He doesn't do too hot when it comes to pep talks. Once he used a speech from *Braveheart*. That, admittedly, was a stretch. But one questionable speech in three years is a pretty good record.

"Okay, boys, tomorrow's our day," Coach finally says. He claps each of us on the back, and we walk out of the gym together into the black evening. It's near eight o'clock, the air crisp with cold. The team's cars are huddled around the field. Mera's—the lone dinosaur—is parked in the middle of the lot.

Christ. I never got her keys back to her. Or gas.

Coach pulls me aside. "What's going on?" He's the real deal; the crease between his brows deepens with worry. "You've got a lot of stuff going on at home. Stuff going on with Luc. A lot of pressure. Is there something I can do?" His cell phone trills, and he clicks it off.

"Don't you need to answer that?" I ask.

He shakes his head. "No. Right now I'm listening to you. Like. Dislike. Like."

We're standing under the hazy light of the parking-lot lamps—our shadows stretch from our feet, long and lanky. I stare down at our spindly legs, carnival-mirror forms.

Coach doesn't say anything.

I try to collect my thoughts. Like. Dislike. Like. But where would I begin?

"You comin' or not?" Luc hollers to us. There's an edge to his voice. The silence is broken.

"Thanks, Coach," I say, and half wave, walking out of the light, the asphalt swallowing my shadow. "I'm cool. Really." But I just want to go back into the light. I don't want to disappear into the sameness of every day.

"Well?" Luc shouts.

Coach nods. "See you tomorrow."

I turn to Luc. "Nah. I gotta get this ecodestructor back to Mera. Christ, she's probably gonna put me on one of her hate-mail lists."

"How'd you get her to lend you the meat vehicle anyway?" Luc asks.

I shrug. It's like she kind of understood that I needed to start my day. Maybe she gets it. If anybody's crazy around here, it's her. So maybe.

"Well?" Luc asks. Irritated. Like being friends with her breaks a code.

"I promised I'd send letters to Congress about animal cruelty. Some PETA thing."

Luc cracks a smile. "Okay." He walks toward me and yanks the back of my neck, leaning into me so we're nose-to-nose, the closest to off-field hugging we'll ever get. "Tomorrow's it. One day. One game. I'll pick you up in the morning." His breath, hot on my face, smells like onion and cilantro.

"Okay," I say, and laugh. It's an easy laugh, like everything has been a big joke. "We got away with it again, Camacho."

"*Guevón.*" Luc laughs, and we slip back into the way things are supposed to be.

I walk to Mera's van. There's a note shoved under the windshield wiper.

Don't even think about returning my van without
filling up the tank. Have to take the bus home and
will probably end up sitting by some freshman who smells
like a decomposed pig. I totally can't believe that
out of millions of sperm you were the quickest.

Total Mera. I sigh and slip behind the wheel and turn on the engine, the gas gauge in the red. Fifteen gallons of gas plus all I owe Luc. I open up my wallet. Empty.

The words itch at the back of my mind—something I can't quite shrug off this time.

You okay, Jake? Do you want to talk about it?

Mera's words.

It's like all these years nobody has ever said that. *You okay, Jake?*

What if that day—the day Dad came home at 7:19 in the morning to find me in the closet, huddled in my own piss and vomit, and Kasey at the bottom of the stairs with a broken arm from falling down—*what if* somebody'd asked, *Are you okay?*

I could've said, *No.*

Maybe I would've said, *Yes.*

But the question, the possibility, would've been there. The open door.

Maybe when I leave the van at her house, we can just talk for a while.

Maybe.

SIXTY-SEVEN IN THE SHADOWS

Friday, 7:43 p.m.

Seven forty-three. Seven plus four is eleven plus three is fourteen minus seven is seven. OK.

"When will you get here?" Kasey asks. "Dad's locked himself up in the garage and is listening to that seventies rock-band stuff, and Mom's in the bedroom pacing back and forth. I think Mom's back on meds. I *hate* it here."

I cradle the phone on my shoulder and turn down Highway 50 to find cheap gas. "I'll be there soon, K. Things just got a little out of control today."

"You were late again," she says. "Did Mom totally embarrass herself today?"

"Nah. She's fine. She'll be fine," I say. "What's the home front like?"

"Weird. Dad in that cool zone, like any second he'll go total Doritos Blazin' Buffalo and Ranch rage."

"Doritos?"

She laughs. "Ran out of Triscuit varieties. With Doritos we're covered probably till you graduate."

"Hope so. You do your homework?"

"Yeah."

"Okay. Tell me about your day." I pull into the station.

"You know, Jake. Everybody who's anybody is going to the party at Mario's tomorrow."

"I'm not."

"You don't count. I need to start upping the maintenance work here."

"No," I say. The numbers spin in a lame attempt to fill up Mera's guzzler. The gas sputters and stops flowing when the numbers hit $19.93. Good number.

I swipe my debit card and look at the statement receipt. My bank account officially has eleven cents in it.

Nineteen ninety-three for gas. Eleven cents left. Good signs. Things are looking up. I exhale, and the pounding in my head settles to a dull throb.

Way better.

"You're such an ass. It's *after* the game. It's not like you'll have anything to think about tomorrow. Come with me."

"Not this weekend," I say. "I told you that."

"I don't even know why I have to ask you about this kind of stuff."

"We've got each other's backs. I'm not going to spend tomorrow night with a bunch of freshmen after the biggest game of the year. Christ, K, don't be such a brat about this."

"Yeah, like you ever do anything but sit in your room."

"Kasey," I whisper. She knows she's crossed the line. "Drop it." Kase is a cool kid but she definitely has her shit moments.

"Okay." She exhales and starts to talk. Half her classmates' ears must be in flames. She goes in bullhorn mode when she gets really riled up, so I move the phone a little bit away from my ear to keep from going deaf.

When I turn on the ignition, the gas gauge barely moves. Christ. For being so pro-animal and environmental, you'd think Mera would ride her bike to school instead of this clunker.

"Are you even listening?" Kase's monologue is coming to an end.

"Yeah, K."

"Will you be home soon?"

"Just gotta drop this van off at Mera's."

"I'll wait up."

"I know."

"Always do."

"Always do." I slip the van into gear and hang up the phone. My stomach cramps and I realize I haven't had anything since this morning's two bites of crumbly biscuits and funky-smelling gravy, so I rummage around Mera's glove compartment and find a stale-looking Luna bar. *Christ.*

When I pull up to her house, two-thousand-watt sensors go off and blanket the driveway in bright white light. They could have a nice marijuana plantation with that kind of lighting. After two minutes, thirty-nine seconds they flick off, leaving the house in quiet darkness except for the dim light that shines behind heavy drapes. *Two thirty-nine. Two plus three is five plus nine is fourteen minus three is eleven. OK.* The wind blows, and I listen to the whisper of dry leaves scuttling across the lawn. I wonder if Mera is home.

Her bedroom light is off.

It's Friday night. Nobody stays home on Friday night. Not even Catherine Margaret Silverman—debate team, chess club, tennis captain, voted Most Likely to Run Out of Ink When Printing a College Résumé—stays home on Fridays.

Maybe Mera's with some orchestra friends.

What *does* Mera do on weekends? What do orchestra kids do on weekends?

Nothing? Like me?

I have soccer. That's my excuse. And off-season I play indoor soccer, then spring league, summer training, back to soccer season. It's just too fucking insane to break routine. The last time I went to a party, I spent most of it outside, lying behind some prickly rosebushes and staring up at the stars. I practically froze my balls off and had to listen to a heavy make-out session and couldn't move because they were right next to me. It took forever for my balls to warm up.

I turn the radio to FM and skip through the stations, looking for something decent. I settle for The X and the Blues Project, listening to the rasp of Gavin DeGraw, and crank it up to an ear-blasting twenty-three.

I think about running out of cash at nineteen ninety-three. Good sign.

If the sensor lights go on. Two more times. I'll knock on Mera's door. Maybe we can just talk—hang out.

Be real.

The lights flick on. I see a cat streak across the driveway. So I start to count the seconds until the lights turn off. One hundred thirty-five seconds.

Just one more time, and I'll knock on the door.

I wait and turn away from the sensor lights, turn off the van, and get out, careful not to make the sensors go off myself. That's cheating.

I'm now sitting on the bumper. Waiting. And I hear the song—the repetition of notes. It's familiar, like one of those culture things we should all know. I should look it up online or something. I close my eyes, practically seeing how the notes slip out her window and drift away on the wind—up to the stars, up to the night.

It's a good sign.

The wind picks up and the driveway is blanketed in white light. I count the one hundred fifty-nine seconds until they turn off and check the time on my cell. 8:29.

The perfect number.

I have one minute to get to the porch.

Or less.

So I rush toward Mera's house until my foot rests on the first step. I glance back at my cell, and just as I look down, the time changes to eight thirty.

Christ.

8:30

Eight thirty. Eight divisors. One, two, five, ten, eighty-three, one hundred sixty-six, four hundred fifteen, eight hundred thirty. Two, five, and eighty-three are prime. Three primes. OK.

I pause. Then the time changes to 8:31 and my mind races.

The sensor lights flick on again. I'd swear I can hear the buzz of energy. My chest tightens and I try to work out the numbers. My stomach cramps and I swallow back the Blueberry Bliss Luna bar that's worked its way up from my lower GI tract.

The tingling starts at the back of my neck.

The buzz of the sensor lights turns into the sound of thousands of crickets rubbing their forewings together—a chirping, piercing noise.

Then the lights flick off again, just after the sharp *zzzzt* sound of what was probably the last living fly before winter hits.

It's gotta be 8:35. Maybe 8:36.

I can't bring myself to look at the time. My head feels fuzzy, like my brain's blood has to work its way through thick layers of tangled spiderwebs. I take my foot off the porch and back away. A shadow moves from behind the front window curtains and pushes them to the side.

The sensor lights flick on again, the buzzing returns.

The explosion hits and everything turns black for a second, a bazillion dots of light like dust motes in my brain. I crouch down and rest my head on the first step, closing my eyes until the dots go away.

The music is gone. I don't know when she stopped playing. Somebody taps on the window—the noise like the pounding of a bass drum.

I swear I can smell burned insect bodies.

My hands tremble and Mera's keys slip from my sweaty palm, thunking on the concrete sidewalk—a deafening sound.

It's all wrong. The time. The numbers. I open my eyes and focus, looking down at the glowing numbers on my cell phone. 8:36.

Just be normal.

Get it together.

The magic is broken. The numbers are too bleary to work out, tangled in the webs in my brain. So I stand and turn away.

"Jake," somebody says, but it's hard to hear anything above the shrill buzzing in my ears—the thumping in my brain.

I escape into the shadows of her neighbor's house at 251 North Elizabeth Street and lie down beneath a tree—dried twigs snagging my soccer shirt. The ground is hard. 251.

Two times five is ten plus one is eleven. OK.

My entire body twitches with cold—chicken-skin arms. I didn't even realize that I've been shivering until now, and I rub my skin, keeping my eyes clenched shut—keeping the dark in, until I can see the numbers again. I fight to clear my head, get the numbers in focus, but when I open my eyes a little, I turn on my side to throw up blueberry acid.

I wait.

And count.

Time slips away, hours pass, until I'm able to get to 991 in my primes; then it's like a maze opens up in my brain, pushing through the fog, revealing the patterns. My breathing comes easier. The numbers take form, and I can go through and make sense of it all.

I sit up and lean my head against the icy siding of the neighbor's house. The webs disintegrate and everything seems clearer. My stomach roars.

I stand up. Slowly.

Don't look back. Don't look at Mera's house.

That would ruin everything.

Tomorrow this will end. I don't need to talk to anybody. I just need tomorrow to be perfect—to end the cycle and put things to rest.

That makes me feel better, knowing I'm less than a day away.

So I work my way home, counting my steps, one step away from touching the flamingo's beak. *Eight hundred fifty-six.* I freeze and wait until the numbers on my phone line up, taking my last step toward the flamingo. *Eight hundred fifty-seven steps at twelve twenty-nine.*

Two primes.

The day ends right.

SEVENTY-ONE FOCUS

Saturday, 12:29 a.m.

Twelve twenty-nine. One plus two is three plus two is five plus nine is fourteen divided by two is seven. OK.

I exhale and brush the flamingo's beak, then run up the porch. I open the door soundlessly and creep inside the black house, making my way up the stairs, avoiding steps four and eight and the creaking floorboard at the top.

"Do you have any idea what time it is?" Light floods the hallway.

"Jesus, Kase. What the—" I shade my eyes, adjusting to the light. "That's just creepy, you know."

"Well?"

"Well what?"

"Do you have any idea what time it is?"

Dumb question.

I *always* know what time it is.

Kasey's standing outside the door to her room, hands on hips, doing this toe-tapping thing that Mom should do.

Dad comes out of the bedroom. "Where've you been?"

"I was with some of the guys, talking about the game tomorrow," I say.

Dad scowls. "Luc's called several times."

"Yeah. He couldn't get me on the cell. But he finally did."

See me, I think. *See the lies. See me.*

Mom calls for Dad. Dad looks at me and nods. "Get some rest. We'll deal with this later." He slips back into the bedroom, shutting the door. I squeeze down the pain that creeps up the back of my neck and rub my arms.

I've never been so cold in all my life.

"Well?" Kasey crosses her arms in front of her ratty bathrobe. I should get her a new one.

I slump in front of her door in the hallway. She hands me a plate of geometric beauty—symmetrical sandwiches that look like turhamken shrines. "Thanks for the food. You saved my life." It takes three bites to down the first one.

Kase hands me a bottle of flavored water. "Luc called four times. He's such a wanker."

I look at my watch.

12:37

Twelve thirty-seven.

I'm so tired. The numbers blur and fade. *FOCUS.*

Twelve thirty-seven.

Fuck. One plus two is three plus three is six plus seven is thirteen.

OK.

"Why are you still up?"

Kase looks at me and rolls her eyes.

"Okay. Dumb question."

"So?" she says.

"So," I sigh, and lean my head against the wall, closing my eyes, letting exhaustion take over. "Tell me about your day."

A stream of moonlight slips through the tear in the black-out blind. For a moment I wonder if the light will erase my image forever.

I have the weirdest fucking ideas.

Kasey's lying next to me in the hallway. We're covered with her princess blankets—the ones she hides in her closet when friends come over since it's not cool to have Cinderella blankets when you're in ninth grade. "Kase," I say, and tap her on the shoulder. "Wake up. Go to bed."

I half carry her to bed and tuck her in, pulling up her curtains so moonlight spills into her room, casting shadows

171

on the walls. The silent street is dimly lit by the soft yellow light of the streetlamp. The yellow light sputters and flashes. My eyes burn from tiredness but I can't sleep, waiting for the sputtering to end.

I stay awake until the sputtering ends and the glow is swallowed by dawn's first light. I turn to my clock.

6:07 a.m.

Christ.

Six-oh-seven. Six plus seven is thirteen. OK. Seven minus six is one plus six is seven. OK. The numbers are working. I close my eyes and think about the game—the release.

The webs disintegrate. I just have to make it through one more day like this. Then I'm free. Later I'll deal with Coach and the scouts and Luc. My stomach knots; the dull pain sharpens.

Today everything will go right again. I can't blow it.

Future.

Scouts.

The game. Twenty-two guys—shit number. Don't count the other team.

Eleven guys. One ball. I push everything aside and rework my brain.

Focus on the game.

We *have* to win. The anxiety I feel is blanketed by a feeling of excitement—hope.

Today I will be normal.

I mentally work my way through the maze of Gorman's players, passing the ball, creating opportunities, feeling light as air.

Goal.

SEVENTY-THREE BEGINNING PERFECTION

"Jake!" Kasey pounds on my door. "Jake, wake up!"

Light floods the room. The frost has melted and my windows drip with last night's cold. I turn to the clock. Saturday, 9:08 a.m.

Nine-oh-eight. Nine plus eight is seventeen. OK. Eight times nine is seventy-two minus nine is sixty-three plus eight is seventy-one. OK.

The door flies open and Luc walks in. "*Guevón.* What's up? We're meeting the team for breakfast. We leave in five. Goddamn, it smells like Teen Spirit in here. Do you *ever* shower?"

I open one eye and look at the clock. Then open the other eye.

9:10

Nine ten. Nine plus one is ten. WAIT. WAIT.

Nine eleven. Nine plus one is ten plus one is eleven. OK.

"I'm not gonna wait around for your lazy albino ass all day. C'mon."

I slip my left foot out from under the covers and count. *One, two, three.*

Fifty-six, fifty-seven—

Right foot. *One, two, three.*

Fifty-eight, fifty-nine.

Up.

9:11

Luc glares and says, "What the . . . Did you not hear me? We're *late.*"

I nod. Counting words. Nine if I count *we're* as one. I think I can.

Nine words. Not OK. Shit.

"And I need some gas money for tonight, okay?"

Nine words. Nine. Fuck. Nine. It's just out there, dangling in front of me. Pinpricks of pain start to climb up my temples.

"Okay, *guevón?*"

Ten, eleven. OK. I sigh.

I nod.

Eleven. Good number.

I hardly notice Luc. He's just taking up space, not time.

Well, a little time. I head to the bathroom. The conditioner has more in it than the shampoo so I spill it out until they're level and step into the shower. *Left, right, left, right.* Lost in the numbers until I hear someone pounding on the door. I drip a little more conditioner out until it's level with the shampoo and shower gel.

"Jacob Daniel! Get out of the shower and downstairs. Now!"

"Thanks, Mr. Martin," I hear Luc say.

I count to one hundred one and turn off the shower, watching as the water drips down my body to the drain—pieces of curly hair swirling in the stream of water.

I stare at the pubes and want to vomit but can't stop staring until the last of them slip into the drain. I squat down and look closer but don't see any more, and I pull myself away from the drain before I begin to count its holes.

Luc pounds on the door again, saying something to the effect that if I don't leave the bathroom right now, he's going to drag me out and hang me by my balls.

"Leave him alone, Luc!" Kasey's voice gets pretty squeaky when she's about to cry. I feel like shit. This isn't her battle. I'm the one who's supposed to look out for her. Not the other way around.

Luc and Kasey really get into it, their voices cutting my concentration, fucking with my numbers. I holler, "Just. Shut. Up. I'll get out when I'm fucking ready to get out. Shut. Up."

My head throbs in time to the drip, drip of the faucet. So I turn the knob tight until the drips stop and I can sit and wait until the mirror defogs on its own. I rest my head on the sink—the cool porcelain feels good against my cheek; the whole place is fogged in steam.

Vapor. Condensation. Mist. Haze.

Water particles.

Bazillions of visible water particles floating in air.

I'm just glad I don't have the urge to count them.

Take that back. I'm just glad they're too small to see to count.

When the air clears, I say, "Coming." I run my fingers through my hair and open the door with both hands.

Luc sits outside my bedroom door, head banging against the doorjamb. He glares at me from underneath the scrunched-up monobrow. I push past him and get dressed, just the way I need to get dressed. Luc can wait. Everything can wait.

"*Guevón*, do you think we can leave sometime today?" he hollers through the door. "It's not like every tomorrow is riding on today. Not at all. Take your time. Can I offer you fucking tea and biscuits?"

He doesn't get that right now is tomorrow and every other day in my life unless I get it right today. I can't afford another day like yesterday, trying to put broken pieces together.

Today has to be perfect.

Magic.

I look at the clock.

10:14

Ten fourteen. One plus one is two plus four is six plus ten is sixteen minus one is fifteen minus one is fourteen minus one is thirteen. OK.

I turn from the clock and walk into the hallway. "Ready."

Luc stares at me, mouth gaping. And I realize he has no idea who I am—his preconceptions of me have evaporated. They're gone.

And so are mine.

I am crazy.

SEVENTY-NINE TRIGGERS

Saturday, 10:15 a.m.

Ten fifteen. One plus one is two plus five is seven. OK.

I skip steps eight and four on the way down, touch the grandfather clock, and go into the kitchen, where Mom slouches next to the sink, clutching a thick coffee cup that looks too heavy for her to hold; her thin fingers look brittle like dried twigs, her eyes vacuums of nothingness.

For a second I don't feel anything but anger. *Stop being a victim. Stop being like that.*

Stop leaving us.

And this is what Dad must feel when he sees me do my weird-ass things—like a fire consumes his insides and burns slowly until all he sees is red.

I won't be Mom. I won't have Dad feel about me like I feel about Mom right now. Parents are supposed to love their kids—be proud of them.

Kasey sits cross-legged on the window seat where she always sits to eat breakfast: a bowl of Honey Nut Cheerios, half a glass of orange juice, and a third of a cup of fruit. She takes a silent bite of cereal and stares at Luc like he's evil incarnate. Dad holds the newspaper in front of his face.

We're silent.

It's like all appearances have been peeled away this past week. I try to go back to where it all started to go bad. If they hadn't done that lame-ass breakfast yesterday; if my memories hadn't been set loose. If Mom hadn't left . . .

What if Mom was a mom . . . just for once?

I shake the thought off and stare at her. But she's gone, so I push the anger away. The burning in my stomach dulls to a tired ache. I start to count events, going back, trying to fix the frazzled wires.

Future.

My future is stuck in the past.

My chest constricts and I count the seconds on the grandfather clock, watching the hand tick around. I turn away when the minute hand inches forward and the second hand is on fifty-nine.

10:16

Ten sixteen. One plus one is two plus six is eight minus one is seven. OK.

Kase is wearing one of my old soccer sweatshirts. "I'll be there early. Everybody's gonna be there, you know." She points to my soccer bag. "Got everything?"

"Yeah."

"Change of clothes?"

"Yeah, Kase. It's not like it's the first time I've packed my soccer bag."

"Okay. Just making sure."

"Thanks." I sigh. Somebody's got to be the mom.

"Got your back," she says.

"Got your back," I say.

She squeezes me hard and smirks with a raisin stuck in her teeth. I crack a smile.

Mom looks up at me with empty eyes. "Jake, honey."

"That's okay, Mom. I get it. You better rest." I push her hair back behind her ears. She always has it covering her face. And she's pretty. She could be really pretty if . . .

Lots of *if*s in this family.

Dad lays his paper on the table. "I'll be there."

He looks at me in a way that erases the craziness for a second—like he's proud for real, not just because he has to say so.

"Thanks, Dad." And my head feels a little clearer. All I need to do is get on the field and everything will go away.

Luc nudges me. "Enough of the Osbornes, okay? Let's go."

I open the door with both hands, then jump into Luc's

car, easing the door shut. He turns the radio up thirteen notches, staring at me from his peripheral vision, as if he's really seen who I am.

I am real.

This is me.

But that's not acceptable and I know it.

The pulsing in my head doesn't get worse. The auras don't come. I'm going to kill out on the soccer field to erase this morning, these past few days, from Luc's memory—to get back preconceptions, because it's way better when people don't know. What people want to see is better than what is before them. It's always been that way, and the only person who has ever shifted that train of thought is Mera.

I've got to learn to move slower, more deliberate. I've got to watch my words so that I don't say something that will eventually cause a tsunami in Asia. Action/reaction. Cause/effect. Everything is under my control if it's all contained.

The numbers are mine.

The spiders are mine.

I *own* them and don't have to explain that to anybody. And after we win today, they'll be sent away because I'll have control.

I look at the time on my watch, and my mind works out the numbers until we pull into Coach's driveway. Luc turns off the radio.

"Okay," Luc says. He looks at me weird, like I'm not

Jake anymore. That bugs the shit out of me because I'm not different. He's just seeing me different.

Perception.

Reality.

"Okay," I say, and open the door.

"Just a sec," Luc says.

I brace myself because I'm not sure how things will be now that he knows about me—the truth—whatever that truth is, because I sure as fuck haven't figured it out yet either. We're walking the line between perception and reality, like too much has gone on the past two days to blow off.

Maybe I can tell him why we need to win—the real *reason.*

Luc leans his head against the steering wheel and looks me in the eyes. "You were right."

Silence. I search through my memories to try to figure out what I could possibly have been right about in the twelve years Luc and I have been friends other than the fact that Aquaman is the biggest pansy-ass superhero with virtually worthless powers.

I clear my throat. "About what?"

"Yesterday and me and my dad."

Exhale. "Nah, man. I was just talking bullshit—"

"Let me say this," he says.

It's just us again. It's time to be real.

Real.

"It's like he's still here, you know? He's this dead

motherfucker that never leaves me alone. Sometimes something just sets me off, triggers it, and I go all bloop tube. What if—" He lowers his voice. "What if he never leaves? That shit freaks me out, you know. Like I can't trust myself. I *can't* be him."

But he is.

And I can't be Mom. But I am.

But for just one more day.

Then the spiders will go away.

"What triggers it?"

Luc shrugs. "I don't know. You. Fuck, man, you and your weird-ass shit. And other shit that shouldn't matter, but just one thing can get me raging. Does that even make sense?"

Every time I'm stuck somewhere, I go back to that day in the closet—the day I first remember the spiders not leaving, figuring out how to get them to by holding fast to the numbers, willing away the sticky webs. Does that make sense?

It's all about the trigger, like a domino that falls and collapses a thousand others. If I can just stop the first one . . . I push the slight tingle from the back of my neck down.

"I don't know," I say, and feel like the biggest oxygen waster on the planet because I can't tell my friend how to not be his dead dad. "I wish I knew." It's like some vacuum has sucked out all the happy air and left us with a future repeating the past.

We're all stuck.

The spiders will go away.

I scratch my neck.

Luc claps me on the back and says, "Shit, M&M. Enough Dr. Phil. Just forget about it. I think this game is getting to my head too much." He practically jumps out of the car. I watch him through the curved windshield. He crunches through the last of the leaf piles on the street like a little kid. He twirls his key chain around his finger and stomps through the gutter, twigs snapping underneath.

Luc returns to the car, tapping the car hood. He rings his thumb and forefinger around his nose. *"Marica,"* he mouths, and grins.

"Assmunch." I ease out of the car, then close the door, shutting the truth inside.

EIGHTY-THREE HAUNTED

Saturday, 10:23 a.m.

Ten twenty-three. One times two is two plus three is five. OK.

We walk up Coach's porch, a tricycle and sand toys scattered everywhere. His wife opens the door and lets us in. The table looks like it was attacked by mad dogs, but she leads us to the kitchen to plates piled high with fruit and wheat toast, scrambled egg whites, and orange juice. "There's more," she says, and smiles.

Coach's daughters hide behind her.

The guys are playing Pro Evolution Wii soccer. Diaz says, "Dude, Martin, when can we play you on the screen?"

I pretend not to notice Luc flinching and turn to him.

"Camacho," I say, "only with you on defense, man," and pretend to give him a big kiss on the ass.

"Ahh, shit. *Que joto,*" Diaz says, and rolls his eyes.

"Hey!" Coach hollers. I didn't even see him sitting in the back corner, holding his rosary. The beads click together when he makes a fist. "Watch your language."

Diaz nods and says, *"Sí, señor."*

The room is blanketed in silence. Coach's wife comes in and discreetly covers her nose with a Kleenex. I inhale. There's nothing smellier than fifteen nervous, sweaty guys who haven't jacked off for the last twelve hours. It's like smelling live aggression. I wonder how we can stand each other.

She says a prayer and sends us on our way. We pile into the cars and drive to school, heaving our bags to the locker room.

I put my earplugs in and crank up Tiger Army's "Ghosts of Memory":

> *This place is poison to my soul*
> *Can't take much more, I'm losing control*

I'm haunted.
Yeah. That's it.
Focus.
I lose myself to the beat of the music, letting the words

skip across my consciousness. I sit on the bench closest to the door, pulling on my left sock, then shin guard. Right sock, then shin guard. I put on my shoes and leave them untied, pulling out the laces so they'll brush the ground. Luc's listening to 3 Pesos. Everybody plugs in.

In here I'm normal. In here it's fine to count, to do the routines, because in here everybody knows the team needs them, and everybody has their own: Kalleres changes his laces out every game. Grundy sleeps with his cleats on the night before. Keller hasn't shaved since the season began.

Here, it's all okay.

The locker room has the familiar musty-towel smell mixed with lemon-scent cleaning detergent and spicy-smelling deodorant. We're quiet when we get dressed. There's something at stake for everybody today.

Everybody.

Coach comes in. He scans the room, looking every one of us in the eyes. "You all know what you have to do. Remember, no one, and I mean no one, comes into our house and pushes us around. This is your game now, gentlemen. And for you seniors, it's your last one, so make it count, because you will remember it for the rest of your lives. Let's get 'em."

We huddle in a tight circle, shoulder to shoulder, head to head, and roar, "Carson, Carson, Carson!"

We follow one another down the hallway to get to the field, falling into pairs—same order, same pairs for the past three years. Luc and I walk behind Diaz and Keller, listening to them bet on Coach's speech. "Bet you don't know the movie, man," Diaz says.

"How much?" Keller asks.

"One Andrew Jackson."

"A Jackson? Feeling pretty sure of yourself, *joto*," Diaz says, and glances back to make sure Coach can't hear him. Diaz is always talking about everybody else being *joto*. It's like everybody's doing "The Rainbow Connection" in the world of Diaz.

"What? And you're not?"

"Fine. Twenty bucks." They shake hands.

"Rudy," Keller says.

"Rudy?" Diaz pauses. "I don't know."

"Look it up."

"Will do."

They walk so close together, their knuckles brush up against each other. Diaz turns back and glares at me, stepping away from Keller. "What's your deal, Martin?"

And I realize we all have secrets.

EIGHTY-NINE TRUTH

Saturday, 2:47 p.m.

Two forty-seven. Two plus four is six plus seven is thirteen. OK.

I unclasp my watch and hand it to Marty, our team manager, who wears it for me during the game. When he was in the hospital because he had appendicitis, he sent his girlfriend to do it for me. Marty's one of the coolest guys I know.

Coach leads us down the hall; we follow in silent reverie, hypnotized by the *click-clack* percussion of our cleats on linoleum. It's the sound of battle.

Before heading outside, we clump together at the end of the hall. We form another circle, then on Luc's command shout, *"Ua! Ua! Ua!"*—the words echoing down the empty hallway, our cleats tap-tapping on the floor, filling up the long corridor like an earthquake.

Luc raises his hand and we stop.

Silence.

Then two by two we head toward the field.

Luc and I slip through the side door, not touching it. Everybody's gone out now. They'll wait for Luc and me so we can make our official entrance.

Luc pulls the door shut behind us, and we're in that place between inside and outside. I feel like we're in an aquarium, just swimming around, slamming our noses against the glass.

"This is it, you know?" Luc says.

"What's it?" I ask.

"This," he says. "The game. State. Three years in a row. Graduating at the end of the year." He looks outside at the line of cars coming from Saliman Road to the parking lot. Full house today for the game.

We're quiet, and I count the cars, trying to let the words in past the numbers.

"There'll be other games and stuff," I say.

Luc shakes his head. "Not like this one."

Luc's right. He's not good enough to play post–high school soccer—except for one of those old-guy city leagues where guys with paunchy guts play, blow out knees, and talk about their glory days and enlarged prostates. We both know that.

So today is it for Luc.

And today is it for me.

Three in a row.

We'll be heroes.

I'm supposed to go to college on some hotshot scholarship. Full ride. Luc'll work at the family business. Sealed destinies.

The spiders wake up when I think about telling Coach and Dad that I can't play anymore—perfection can't be repeated. And I'd rather give up a lifetime of tomorrows of soccer to have normal. Normal.

I clear my throat and try to think of the right words.

For a second that veil of ever-macho Camacho has slipped away and he's like me: scared shitless.

Maybe I'm not such a freak.

Luc holds out his fist, and I tap it with mine, like when we were little, returning to the time before this.

"One more time," he says.

"One more time," I say.

He cuffs me on the neck and laughs, opening the door to head out to the field, leaving us behind. I hesitate, stuck in that doorway, hoping that somehow it can come together here in the space between inside and outside.

"After you, M&M." Luc holds the door open;

November's chill enters our glass bubble.

I walk outside and watch the door close behind us and hate that I didn't say anything real to him.

The crowd roars when we take the field. I look up at the sea of people wearing blue bonnets and laugh. Only Luc could get an entire student body and faculty to wear bonnets. We pull our bonnets out and put them on and the crowd goes nuts.

Luc turns to me. "We are air, Martin. We are air." He bends down and takes a blade of grass, crosses himself, and kisses the blade before letting it fall back to the field.

And I get that. I get that everything Carson City breathes today is because of us. We are a reason—*the* reason.

But what if we lose?

The thought snags on a nerve in my brain, then spreads like an electric storm throughout my whole head. *What if we lose?*

Fuck.

I'm stuck—stuck until I can tear the thought out. I tie my shoes when I hit the halfway line, then double-knot them. My head clears. The routine clicks in—a place where I can do it in front of a thousand people.

No hiding.

Because this is where the magic works. Where it's accepted.

I run down the halfway line laterally, stop, move forward

three steps, and repeat until I complete five rotations, ending up on the opposite side of the field, facing the bleachers, right where the penalty box begins.

The ref blows his whistle, so I loop around the goal and return to where the team is huddled. Luc's getting ready to call the coin toss.

"Heads," I say.

Luc nods. "Heads." He looks at me like I'm Jacob Martin, the last few days erased. He believes in me, in the magic. He knows I'm right when I call heads because we can't lose.

The *what if*s have evaporated.

We huddle one last time around Coach, and he says, "Being perfect is about being able to look your friends in the eye and know that you didn't let them down, because you told them the truth."

Luc and I lock eyes.

What truth? I wonder. Because it seems to me like there are a million truths out there, depending on who tells them.

"And that truth is that you did everything that you could. There wasn't one more thing that you could've done. Can you live in that moment, as best you can, with clear eyes and love in your heart? If you can do that, gentlemen, then you're perfect."

Luc grabs my fist in his. "Truth!" he shouts.

The team shouts, "Truth!" after him.

"Okay, boys," Coach says, tucking his recycled Hollywood speech in his pocket. "Kick the hell out of that ball!"

And that's the best thing I've ever heard Coach say—not borrowed from *Friday Night Lights* or anybody else's script. So today I play for Coach.

Today I play for Luc.

Because this is the day they will always remember—the day we were perfect.

NINETY-SEVEN MAGIC

Saturday, 5:27 p.m.

Marty shouts to me over the roar of the crowd.

Five twenty-seven. Five times two is ten plus seven is seventeen. OK.

The air tastes like snow—sagebrush and snow. The Sierras are completely covered in clouds, leaving us with a gray-blue late afternoon. Balls of saliva dry in the corners of my mouth, and I gulp down the water Marty tossed me from the sideline. Second overtime.

Fuck.

We collapse to the grass. Marty, our manager, and some other guys are pounding on our legs, keeping the blood pumping. Field lights go on with a hum, and we are flooded in light.

Coach weaves in and out among us, his rosary beads clacking in his hands.

Magic.

Magic.

We're all looking for it.

The stands are full. Everybody huddles together, sipping on the watery hot chocolate the snack shack sells. They still wear bonnets, the ones that say *%#@ GORMAN, over earmuffs, hoodies, and heavy hats.

I squeeze my eyes shut and listen to the pound of the drums and the band playing our fight song. I listen to the beating of my heart, blocking out everything until the only sound I hear is the one that comes from within.

I turn on my stomach, the grass tickling my chin, and open my eyes. Gorman's players are huddled together, jumping up and down, an impenetrable wall.

Coach calls us together, and we limp into our huddle. I look over my shoulder at the Gorman players, jumping, jumping, huffing.

"I can't get through," Kalleres says. "I swear to God there are more of them than us on the field."

Luc rubs sweat out of his eyes.

I readjust my headband. "Move Luc up. They're just playing defense. Like some kind of pansy-ass stalemate.

They *want* penalties."

One, two, three, four, five . . . Our breaths come out in ragged gasps.

"No penalties. Penalties is like shooting craps. The best team does *not* win." Coach's rosary beads click like marbles. He stares each of us in the eyes. "*You* are the best out there. *You* need to win this right here, right now."

"That leaves us totally open on the defense," Keller says, then pauses. "But it'll work. It can work."

Coach nods. "Keller and Grundy, you're on your own down there. You've got to be the whole defense because I'm pulling Camacho up to the front line. Kalleres, Martin, Camacho, and Randolph, you will score. I don't want the ball to go past the halfway line. It's all on our end, and we will pound the ball until it goes into the net."

"No more waiting," I say. I hate waiting on somebody else's terms.

The ref blows his whistle. Our team huddles up. "CAR-SON! CARSON! CARSON!" we chant together, then head to our positions. Luc moves up next to me.

"Let's end this fucking thing," I say. "I'm wrecked."

"Okay, M&M, time to do our thing."

And this time, when we're on the field, the magic comes. We cast shadows from the bright glow of field lights, and it's like there are twenty-two of us dancing with the ball. *Twenty-two. Two minus two is zero.*

No numbers.

No time.

Just the field, the ball, and the magic.

I run laterally along the line and push between Kalleres and Randolph, back-passing the ball to Luc, who powers it into the goalpost, bouncing back into the mass of Gorman defense. They're rattled.

I zigzag between our shadows and wonder if it's me or the shadow that brings the magic, because for just a second I feel like my two-dimensional me makes more sense, elongating and compressing, tapping the ball back and forth in this timeless form because shadows show no age.

The ricochet of the ball against the goalpost brings me back from the shadows to the field. "Martin, where the fuck are you?" Luc is shouting, and I shake my head, counting my steps to prepare for their goalie's kick.

And we dance. Gorman and our shadows dance. The ball never goes past the halfway line.

The time ticks away, and Coach waves his arms up and down on the sidelines shouting, "One minute! One minute!"

Luc receives a sideways pass from Kalleres and pauses for a second, right outside the penalty box. He has a clear shot, but flicks it back to me, leaving Gorman's players out of position. I pivot on my right and power the ball with my left, the ball curling around the goalkeeper into the net.

Magic.

ONE HUNDRED ONE FREEDOM

When the ref whistles, I collapse to the ground, breathing in the earthy sweet smell of grass. It tickles the side of my face, so I turn around on my back and squint in the glare of the lights; the first flurries of snow are beginning to fall.

The entire team forms a circle around me—a moat to keep things away. I'm protected in this bubble and can feel my entire body fill with warmth.

Elation.

That's what this is: a moment of total freedom, like the Exodus. My brain is spider free.

I don't even give a shit about the time.

It worked. Magic number three *worked*.

The bench carries Coach out to the field on their shoulders and the circle is broken. It feels as if the whole school has run out onto the field in a crushing wave.

I roll away, covering my head with my arms. I squeeze my eyes shut and roll until I clear the crowd, hitting the goalpost, leaving the frenzy in the middle of the field. The cheerleaders carry the water out and with help dump it on the team. I watch and try to see what is, not what I expect.

Marty looks like he's personally responsible for our team's winning the World Cup. He's soaked in icy water, holding a soggy-looking clipboard. Coach looks up at the near-empty stands and waves at his wife and girls, who are jumping up and down. Luc looks up to the sky and makes the sign of the cross—smiling for real, like he feels the joy that I feel.

I feel *part* of this, like I'm real.

Diaz and Luc jump up and down, arms clasped around each other with their girlfriends holding on. Kalleres and Grundy do their weird winning jig they made up a couple of years ago; they're joined by a whole crowd of people who copy it. Keller watches Diaz and Luc and nudges in. Soon the entire team is hugging and jumping in a big circle—kind of like an impromptu chorus line.

Dad waves at me, a huge smile pasted on his face. He's wearing the Carson soccer sweatshirt I got for him last Christmas. I've never seen him wear it before, and it makes him look much younger. I run over to him, weaving my way through the throng of students.

Dad wraps his arms around me and I feel so good. "Great game, son. Great game." I know this is the closest he'll come to saying *I love you*.

But I guess that's okay, too.

"Thanks, Dad," I say.

Nothing can go wrong; everything is perfect right now, in this moment.

Dad looks at his watch and digs keys out of his pocket. "Celebrate, Jake. Enjoy the moment."

"I will." I try to hold on to that hug, his warmth. I try to ignore the cold feeling that chills my stomach while I watch him head for the parking lot.

Mera sits in the stands, back straight, hair pulled back in a tight ponytail—so blond that she almost looks bald. She watches the crowd. Always watching. Never joining. And she looks sad. Maybe because she can't be down there with them; maybe because she has chosen not to. I work my way toward her. Because she can be part of this. Right now.

I'm almost to Mera when Kasey rushes to me with a gaggle of friends. She jumps into my arms and wraps hers around my neck smelling like Heiress perfume and Altoids. Potent combo. The air tastes minty-fruity.

"I can't believe how absolutely intense that was!"

"So amazing," her friend Lisa, famous for inappropriately

breaking the crush-on-somebody's-big-brother random rule, says.

"Hi, ladies," I say.

Kasey's friends all look like bobbleheads, nodding and giggling. Lisa turns purple when I smile her way.

It's all about momentum—keeping the joy alive. I see the team gearing up to go to the locker room, clean up, go to dinner, then party, party, party. Everybody's happy. They make it look so easy.

It *is* easy because the spiders are gone.

Maybe I'll go to the parties. My head feels good—clear. It looks like everybody is having so much fun. I could do that. Have fun like that.

I walk forward with Kasey attached to my neck, her skinny legs swinging back and forth, her toes brushing against my shoes. "Kase, I'll be out late. I'll call Dad and tell him I'm staying at Luc's, okay?"

I can't remember the last time I've spent the night at someone's house, and I feel my stomach tighten a little. There's a familiar tingling in my neck. It's like I'm flipping through mental snapshots of Luc's room—a total pigsty. I don't even know where his stupid clock is. The tingling changes to a throb and I try to splatter the spiders inside my brain.

No.

But the feeling goes away as quick as it came. Maybe

some kind of aftershock. Because they're gone. Today is perfect.

Everything's perfect.

Everything's so *normal*.

Stop.

Stop.

It's like listening to the click of a hammer being cocked to chamber the round.

I'm not going to do this.

But the harder I resist, the more I feel like going home— going back to where I can do what I need to do.

I don't need to do anything. Today was magic. The spiders have to go away.

When I think about Luc's room, the pain surges. I dart around thoughts, grasping onto one that will keep me in the safe zone.

I won't stay at Luc's. I'll just stay out and party and get home. That way I start and end the day right. That's important. It makes sense. It's how the magic works. I have to finish what I started. If I don't, the win won't matter.

I sigh, relieved I'll still be like everybody else—just partying, having a good time.

The pain subsides.

"Kase," I say, and pry her fingers loose from my neck. "The team's waiting. It's time to celebrate."

She lets go and slides down until her feet touch the

ground. "That's great," she says. "So great." She clears her throat. "You gonna be out all night tonight?"

"Awhile. Why?"

"No reason," she says. "Just, um, wondering."

Marcy butts in. "She's staying the night at my house."

Kase nods.

"Good," I say, distracted by all the people walking by, patting me on the back. So far, twenty-four. *Twenty-four . . . Two plus four is six. Four minus two is two. OK.* Kase keeps talking. "Cool," I say, and feel like I'll end up being the asshole brother after Kase takes one of those chick mag quizzes about how well guys listen.

"You hear me?" Kase asks. Marcy pinches her arm.

"I hear you," I say. *Thirty-two, thirty-three . . .* pats on the back. Kase is staring at me like I'm supposed to say something. I think the social hierarchy is way more complicated in the female gender than in the male. It would probably be a decent conversation topic with Mera.

Luc waves me over. He, Diaz, and Keller are still doing a cancan kick dance. I laugh. They kick me the game ball. "It's yours, man. You deserve it!"

This is so easy. Laughing.

I pick up the ball and toss it to Kasey. "You deserve it. It's yours."

Her friends sigh together and titter. "Ohmygod, ohmygod, ohmygod he's so so dreamy," Lisa says.

Kasey elbows her but I can tell she's beaming.

I wave. "Call you later?"

"Yeah. Keep your phone on," she says. "Got your back," she says.

"Always," I say, and run toward the guys as I catch a last glimpse of Mera. I wave at her, and she smiles and waves back. I hope she's coming to the party too.

ONE HUNDRED THREE NORMALCY

Saturday, 5:43 p.m.

Five forty-three.

I stare at the numbers.

"Hey, Luc," I holler after him, jogging to catch up. "It's five forty-three." Just a time of day, like any other time of day. *Five forty-three.*

Luc waits for me and we walk in the side door together. It's the last time we'll be here—like this, anyway. He picks me up and bear-hugs me, his laughter filling the space. When he puts me down, he opens the door, pauses, then closes it again. "I hope this feeling never ends, you know? Like I could feel like this forever."

"We can. We will." Because I *am* normal.

Luc laughs. "Okay, Mr. Time in a Bottle. Whatever you say. You *are* Magic Martin."

We bump knuckles. Luc inhales. I reach for the door, my hand hovering over the handle. I pull my hand back, my fist balled, trembling.

I am normal now. The spiders are gone.

My neck itches.

"After you, man." Luc holds open the door.

My chest feels tight, but the feeling disappears as quickly as it came. "Last time."

"Last time."

I take out my new crew and a pair of jeans. I don't remember the last time I got new clothes and shove them to my nose, inhaling the smell.

I exhale.

They smell like Tide—not that awful plastic new-clothes smell. They've been washed a couple of times—the collar isn't a perfect V shape. Kase *definitely* is the best kid sister on the planet. While digging in my bag for socks and shoes, I find two notes.

It's like opening a Choose Your Own Adventure card. "If you win, open blue envelope with green writing. If you lose, open green envelope with blue writing." Mom wrote a nice card, real nice. It kind of makes me want to go home and celebrate with them.

Kase won't be there.

Mom won't be there—not really.

And Dad will have taken off his sweatshirt and gotten old again.

I rub my neck. "Join the party!" Luc yanks on my ear and I wince. It's a good distraction.

Then Diaz and Keller do some kind of retro-eighties "Celebration!" song.

How could I have *not* seen this before?

Everybody else joins Kalleres and Grundy in their weird victory dance. We're a pair of legs short of becoming the Rockettes.

Radio City Music Hall, here we come.

I look at Diaz and Keller and laugh. Are they in love?

If I didn't want to spend the rest of my senior year in traction, I'd consider asking them about it. But I shrug it off and rub my neck, willing the pain to go away. I close my eyes and imagine the after-game feeling. That's how I need to feel right now. That's how I'm *supposed* to feel right now.

Coach comes in and says, "Gentlemen, it's time for dinner!"

That's a relief. Dinner. A table. One spoon, fork, knife, and food. I must be hungry, that's all. I follow Coach out of the locker room and sit next to him. He claps me on the back. "I'm proud. This is the opportunity for you, Jacob. Maybe even play pro. But that doesn't matter because you get to study. You can be *anything*."

Now, I think, is not the time to tell him I won't play anymore. We had our three championships. I'm done. I close my eyes and lean my head against the brick wall. I'll have to call Mera to see if I can join her ultramarathon group.

I feel the magic fizzling—like I need something to bring it back. I open my eyes and stare at the floor tiles—bright white with flecks of gray. I avert my eyes from the tiles; the temptation to count the thirty-seven to the door, seventy-nine to the end of the hall, is tickling my brain. I scratch my neck and stare straight ahead. In front of me is a trophy case filled with gold trophies, photos, hall of famers, and ribbons. Nothing balanced—nothing to make sense of it all.

I scan the hallway until I see the clock and wander to it. *Stop. Just stop.*

I don't need the time. I'm not supposed to need this anymore. But I'll just make sure my watch and the clock are synchronized. No big deal.

6:12

Six twelve. Six plus one is seven minus two is five. OK. Six plus two is eight minus one is seven. OK. Six divided by two is three minus one is two. OK. Twelve times six is seventy-two plus one is seventy-three. OK.

The tingling stops and I stare until the second hand hits twelve, turning just in time to follow the guys out to our cars.

The magic. The guys still have it. It's like fairy dust that

210

has settled on their shoulders and remains there.

Tick-tock, tick-tock.

Fuck.

It's okay. It's just gonna take a little bit for it to stay. I feel a tightening in my throat and burning in my eyes. *I've done my part. I made the deal. How come it's not working?*

It's working. It has *to work.*

"Hey! M&M! Are you coming today or what?"

I pull my eyes from the clock and follow them outside. The flurries have turned into real flakes—thick flakes that stick to our shoulders and on our tongues. There's already a skiff of snow on the asphalt, making the parking lot look like a photo negative.

The games are over.

They don't need my numbers anymore.

The magic.

They've got it, so I need to stay with them. Maybe with them I won't need the numbers either. Maybe with them I can be *normal*.

B'Sghetti's has a huge Carson Soccer banner hanging in the window. I sit facing Carson Street with the clock to my left. I can just see it out of my peripheral vision so I have to turn my back a little more; it's gone. Behind me. The numbers are gone.

Tonight I'm partying.

Bowls of salad are brought to us with steaming plates

piled high with pasta and sauce. Luc passes the food to me so I can serve myself first. His eyes flash something— something different.

Pity?

No way. There's *no fucking way* Luc feels sorry for me. When I look back at him, though, the look is gone. He's just Luc.

I'm paranoid.

The restaurant is packed with half the school. We devour the food. I have three helpings, then sit back to wait for dessert. The scouts sit at a table in the corner.

Coach calls them over and introduces them to me. They both say they'll be calling the following week when things settle down.

"Great game, Jacob," says the one with acne scars and bright red hair. His shirt fits tight across his chest. I can almost hear the buttons screaming, *Hold on! Hold on!*

But buttons don't scream.

I rub my eyes and nod. "Thanks," I say, and pretend to not notice Luc bristling beside me.

There is absolutely nothing remarkable about the other scout except for the Maryland pin on his tie. That's enough to make any soccer player in the country pay attention. He holds out his hand. "Good game, Mr. Martin. We'll be talking next week."

"Sure," I say, and turn back to my pie.

Pie.

I love pie. A triangular piece of happiness. Three sides. Symmetrical. Everything works, eating a piece of pie.

I take my last bite and chew three times on my left, two on my right, then swallow, taking my napkin from my lap and placing it on the plate dead center. I put my silverware on top, starting with my knife, then fork, then spoon, and push the plate away from me two inches.

The table explodes in applause. "It's about time, man," Luc says. "We thought you'd never be done."

I didn't even notice that everybody else's plates had been cleared away and Coach was sipping a cup of coffee. The players pound the table and start to chant, "Speech! Speech! Speech! Coach Sanchez has the floor! Speech! Speech!"

Coach stands amidst the thunder of applause and smiles, trying to keep his lip from quivering. "I'm proud of you," he says. "All of you." Then he sits down and crosses his arms in front of him.

Great speech.

Then Luc talks about what it's meant to be on the team and be the team's captain. His voice swells with pride when he says, "Third championship in a row. Good luck next year without me."

The team pounds the table, silverware jingling across. I reorganize my plate and silverware more times than I want to count.

It's over. Time to go. So I pile into Luc's car, this time with Amy and Tanya along for the ride. Luc turns the radio up fourteen notches.

I dig my fingernails into my legs and work the numbers to be okay.

Fourteen. Four plus one is five. OK. Four minus one is three. OK.

But it's still fourteen.

Not OK.

"Where to?" Luc asks, his hand working its way up Amy's thigh at lightning speed.

"Mario's," both Tanya and Amy say at the same time. "Like, where else?" Amy says.

Luc looks at me in the rearview window and raises his eyebrow.

"Mario's," I choke out and turn away from the radio, trying to ignore the pain that's creeping up my neck.

I tap the cell phone in my pants pocket. I'll just call Kase later—just to check on her.

Because today I'm normal.

ONE HUNDRED SEVEN COMFORT ZONE

Saturday, 9:17 p.m.

Nine seventeen.

I stare at the watch face and twirl it around my wrist so I can't see it. Habit. Just a habit.

We can hear the thrum of the bass about a mile away. Luc says, "Yeah. This isn't gonna last long. Mario's such a dumbass."

I flip open my cell phone.

"What's up, *guevón*?"

"Just got to check on Kase," I say.

"That's so sweet." Tanya swoons.

Kase answers all giggly. There's lots of noise in the

background. "Where are you?" I ask.

"Watching movies at Marcy's, okay, Jake?" Kasey slurs her words.

"Are you drunk?"

"No, Jake."

"K, what's going on?"

"I'm perfect, big bro."

"'Big bro?' What?" I try to not sound too much like Dad and not too much like the psycho me that's ready to ooze out all over the place. I say, "Okay, tell me about your day." I need to hear something, *anything*. I need to get things back to normal, *my* normal, just for a second.

"Call you later," she says. The line goes dead.

Call you later.

Before I have a chance to call her back, Tanya's dragging me out of the car. We park a couple blocks away and walk with the forming crowd toward Mario's. He's sitting outside on the porch on a lounge chair wearing swimming trunks and a Hawaiian lei. "Get lei'd, guys," he says.

So original.

A couple of football players man the door. "Nice job, gentlemen," they say when we walk in, draping flowers around our necks.

"You rocked, Martin," says Filpatrick. He's easily the biggest guy in school and could be a total jerk—football player, homecoming king, student-body president, advanced classes, way too perfect, so he's gotta be the school asshole who steals lunch money from the science club. But he's not. He's a great guy.

We shake hands and he steps away from the front door, doing a little bow. "VIPs tonight, guys. Live it up. No cover for you."

"Thanks," I say.

He and Luc embrace—two captains, two great guys. "Ladies first," Luc says, and steps aside for Amy and Tanya to go ahead.

Amy glares at me and clears her throat. "Oh. Yeah. Sorry." I move away from the front door.

Luc rolls his eyes. "Nice, *caballero*, real nice."

I shrug and walk into a fog of pure stench: fermented *something*, sickly sweet perfume, and the musty smell of hormones. The smoke coming from the basement is definitely not burning oregano. And all of a sudden I don't want to touch anything. Everything seems filthy, seedy.

Like everything here will infect me with some kind of flesh-eating bacteria.

My stomach churns. I shove my hands into my pockets to avoid looking at the time.

I don't need it.

Mario's mom's dishes chatter in the china closet in time to the music. Luc pushes me forward and we move to where everyone's dancing, stopping at the bathroom to get a cup full of red fruity shit from the tub.

I squat down and stare at the tub.

People are drinking stuff that comes from a bathtub.

Bathtub uses: cleaning disgusting filth off sweaty bodies, pubic hair catchers, sex, and now red passion juice.

Luc shoves a cup in my hands, the sticky liquid sloshing over the sides. *"Salud!"* he says, and steers me toward what looks like the heart of mayhem. Lindsay Jones is passed out on the coffee table where a group of kids are playing poker, littering her body with the chips. Every now and again somebody leans down and says, "Yep. Still breathing."

We weave around tangled couples and step over some kid's underwear. The only thing I can think about is premature ejaculation.

Premature ejaculation. Stained pants and underwear.

Will I do that?

No.

I can do this. This is what normal does. Normal goes to parties and makes out and gets a hand job. Normal.

And the pain returns to the back of my neck, the webs are being woven, and I begin to feel the fog.

I glance at my watch. Just curious. Nothing more.

9:49

Nine forty-nine. Nine minus four is five plus nine is fourteen minus four is ten minus nine is one. Fuck.

I rub my eyes, sure I see Kasey with a group of friends

heading upstairs. "Kasey!" I holler, pushing through the crowd to get to her. "What are you doing here?"

Kasey giggles.

"Fuck, Kase. I told you *not* to come here." The guy who was holding her elbow disappears into the bobbing dancers. I crane my neck to get a good look at him, but everybody looks the same. "Goddamnit."

"You're embarrassing me," Kasey says in a half-drunken stupor.

I grab the red cup out of her hand and dump the contents into a planter.

"Jake," Luc says, "lighten up. We're all here to look out for her."

"I don't need *anybody* to look out for me." She says this while stumbling backward into Marcy and her gaggle of friends.

"You," I say, "sit here. In this corner. You don't move. And when I say it's time to go, we go."

Luc waves Kalleres and Grundy over.

"Babysitting? Fuck no, Luc," Grundy says.

"You're juniors. I'm a senior. You take care of Kasey. Got it?"

Some guy with them smirks.

I grab his collar and slam him against the wall. "Don't even *think* about it, or I'll kill you. Who the fuck are you, anyway?"

"Lighten up, man," Grundy says. "We've got her, okay? Go have fun for once, already."

Kasey's friends do a synchronized "Oooh-ahhh-oooh" sound.

"Yeah. And you wonder why nobody asks me out. I'm Crazy Jake Martin's little sister."

They all sit in a corner near the staircase. Kalleres and Grundy pull up folding chairs and sit in front of the girls. Luc pushes me back into the party and the wall of dancers.

Crazy Jake Martin.

The webs spin faster, wrapping around my nerve cells.

No. Nonononononono.

I look around. I'm not screaming. But this isn't supposed to be. Today I was magic. Today I gave it all up for them—to make things right.

Fuck.

Thick webs coil around my temple arteries, strangling them with poison—covering my brain. I've gotta work out the numbers before I see the auras. I look around and push between people, trying to make my way to a free beanbag in the corner near an open window.

And there she is: Mera Hartman.

At a party.

She's wearing tight jeans, just-right-tight, and a soft green sweater. She comes and sits next to me on the beanbag, and I feel a gush of relief. The pain recedes.

220

"Who're you here with?" I ask.

She looks around. "From the looks of it, half the high school, all inebriated and ready to do things they hope to God won't get put in the yearbook."

I laugh. "You came alone?"

"Technically, yes. But I'm not alone now."

"Wow. Aren't you breaking some kind of major social code that dictates that one should not go to a gathering of drunk people alone?"

She laughs. "If you haven't caught on, I'm not big on social codes."

That's what makes Mera an offense to nine-tenths of the student body: She's fearless. Nobody in high school should be so confident—so real. No masks. No hiding behind anything. It's unsettling.

"Good game," she says, interrupting my thoughts.

"Perfect," I say.

"Well, I wouldn't go *that* far."

That bothers me. It was *perfect. That's why I'm normal.*

"Almost perfect," she says.

Almost won't work.

Fuck.

I try to focus on *now*. My mind begins to reel back, though, through the tape of the day, back to the game. *Where was it not perfect?*

Mera raises her glass. "Cheers."

"You drinking that stuff?" I ask.

"Are you kidding? But if you carry a half-empty cup around in your hand, nobody will ask you about it."

"Good tip. You come to lots of these things?"

"Obviously more than you."

"Well, that's not too hard to do. This is my second party." I scream to her over the noise of the party, and a couple of people look our way. I can feel my face get warm.

"No way," Mera says.

"Way," I say.

"I'm glad you're here, then," Mera says. "I'm glad I came."

"Me too," I say.

"Me too, as in you're glad *you're* here or you're glad *I* came?"

"Both, I guess." A giggling sophomore falls on top of us. Mera and I push her up on her feet, back into the mob of dancers. She's got about five to ten minutes before she begins puking or totally passes out.

Mera turns to me. "You guess?"

"Honestly? I really don't want to be here. I'm just trying to do the normal thing. Maintenance." That's what Kase would say.

I look over and see Kasey's friends consoling her. Her shoulders shake with sobs. Tonight we're breaking all sorts of "rules for normal."

Mera laughs. "Normal? Maintenance? I read this quote on a napkin once. It said: 'Be yourself. Everyone else is already taken.'"

"Wise napkin, huh?"

"Definitely."

But she doesn't know what being me is. And I think about Coach's speech about truth, looking people in the eye. I turn away.

"Jake, you're not like them. That's a good thing, you know," Mera says.

"How do you know that? That I'm not like them?" I ask.

"Because I've known you since I was old enough to know things. A friend once said that to me—a friend I'd forgotten I had."

I feel like a phony. Because she doesn't know. Not *really*. Truth is, sometimes all I want is normal. What's so bad about being like them anyway? They have fun. They party. They live in the world they created; they have control.

I scoot the beanbag closer to the window, thankful for the icy breeze coming through, and start to count red plastic cups, wondering how long I'll have to be here before I can leave. Mera sits closer and we watch the party like we'd watch a movie in our outside-looking-in, two-dimensional existence.

And for the first time in a long time, not on a soccer field or in my room, I feel almost normal.

I close my eyes and feel a faint brushing of lips on mine. "Mer—" I open my eyes. Tanya grabs my hands and yanks me up, pulling me to her. We sway back and forth on the dance floor, her hands in my back pockets, holding on until not even air can fit between our bodies.

She practically decapitates me, yanking my head down, shoving her tongue in my mouth—her tongue ring, one I'd never noticed for whatever reason, clicking against my teeth, rolling around my tongue. "C'mon, Jake, let's find a place to *be*." I can taste her fruit-punch saliva on the corners of my mouth and a tinge of clove cigarettes.

She shoves my hand up her shirt, slipping it under her

bra, and cups it around her tit, rubbing my fingers across her hardened nipple. "C'mon, Jake. Let's go."

My heartbeat thunders in my head. The room is spinning, swirling like that old merry-go-round, and everything looks like funhouse mirror reflections. Tanya's body is elongated, deformed. Her chin dripping down to her collarbone. Behind her, Luc and Amy dance in squat, dwarf bodies. I squeeze my eyes shut and try to push back the glowing lights. Red, blue, green.

Christ. I've got to go before my head explodes and all the colors ooze out.

"Jake," Tanya says. "Over there." She motions to a closed door.

I look around and feel Luc's breath in my ear before I hear the words. "Thank me later."

The universal fix-all for any guy: sex. Instead of feeling the surge of blood heading south, my body feels like somebody just threw a bucket of icy water on it.

"C'mon, Jakey," Tanya says, and walks away.

God, when I was little my *mom* called me Jakey. My mouth feels like it's exploding with fungal abscesses that spread, swelling my tongue until it suffocates me.

I crane my neck, looking for Mera, and see her slip out the front door. She doesn't even look back. The girl who might be my only real friend in my life is gone.

Five years ago, I chose Luc, and now that's got me here:

in one of Mario's famous storage/sex closets with Carson High's horniest, hottest chick.

This is *normal*. This is what I want.

Somebody shoves me into the closet. The door slams behind us. I hear a click.

The closet is cloaked in blackness except for a tiny streak of light that comes in from the hallway. Tanya grabs my hand and pulls me down to the floor with her, shoving shoes and coats out of the way. "Comfy?" she asks.

"I'll be right back, Jakey. Take care of Kasey. I have to go. Look at the time. I'll be back when the hands on your watch match up to the hands I drew."

The walls close in and squeeze, shutting my airway, constricting my blood vessels. I inhale but can't get any air. I'm trapped under the weight of darkness and fumble around the closet looking for any source of light. I've gotta see something, *anything*. I stand up . . .

. . . pushing myself off the ground, my hand grazing the thick rat tail. I jump back, knocking over a box of Halloween decorations, shiny plastic clown masks, glow-in-the-dark skulls.

I bang my head against the slanted ceiling, a sharp pain searing down my body like electric pulses. The closet smells musky and pungent with a hint of Tanya's floral perfume. I inhale the . . .

> . . . *death smell and gag, throwing up macaroni-and-cheese dinner. "Mom!" I holler. But I know she's not here. The painted hands don't line up with my watch hands. I push hard on the Indiglo light, the button digging into my finger. Make the numbers work to keep Kasey and me safe. I just need . . .*

. . . light. "Turn on a fucking light." I graze my hand across the slanted ceiling, feeling for a light. My head spins. I inhale again, gasping for air, and slump to the floor, cradling my head in my arms, trying to keep out the smells and sounds, to get back the numbers—just a piece of magic to last long enough to get out of here before I do something totally humiliating like black out in my own vomit. I scrape my tongue along my teeth, pushing off the taste of fruit punch. *Focus. Focus. Focus.*

I close my eyes and pretend I'm not locked away.

Just pretend I'm in bed. Just stare at the watch.

I need the numbers. So I squeeze my head between my knees, hoping to stop the spinning webs—hoping to curb the pain.

Tanya rubs my cheek with ragged nails. "What's up, Jake?"

Her voice is different. It's doesn't have that hoarse,

sex-you-up sound to it anymore. I massage my temples, try-ing to hold the auras back, just for a few more minutes.

Look at the time. Focus on the numbers. Just pretend . . .

. . . everything's okay. Tanya's sitting next to me. "What's up? It's not like they rent these by the hour, you know. Mario's closets are in high demand." She laughs. But it's a nervous laugh, like she doesn't want to be here either. "I've got a condom if that's what you're worried about." I hear a rustle. "They're called Sex Bull condoms. How lame is that? I guess it's all pretty lame when you get right down to it."

The second hand ticks, ticks, ticks. Tick-tock. Tick-tock.

The numbers blur, then come clear again. I listen to Tanya. And for once it's like she's being real. The suffocat-ing weight of the closet lifts for a second.

In elementary school, Tanya was a Girl Scout. She won prizes for selling cookies and wore knee-high socks and brown skirts. She was real.

What are we all so afraid of?

I almost kiss her hand, then jerk my head back because I can still taste the fruit punch and acid, and I'm afraid my tongue might've turned black by now, and my mind searches for numbers and patterns.

The glow of red and yellow has gotten stronger. It won't be long before everything goes black. I've just got to get out of here and find a place to be. I've got to do the routine to get things right.

I need the magic.

Counting lights. House lights, streetlights, headlights. I can count. I can walk. That'll buy me time. It always does.

Tanya pulls my face to hers and tries to pry my clenched teeth open with her tongue. "C'mon, Jakey," she says in a singsong, nails-on-the-chalkboard voice. Not only am I limp but I also feel like I've got fishing line with weights hanging from my balls.

Premature ejaculation? Try premature impotence.

I peel her off me, squeezing my eyes shut to try to keep the lights away just for a second longer. "No," I say.

I hear the garage door clatter open and a slamming door. A key rattles in the door. "Mama! Open the door!" The hands don't line up with the painted ones.

7:19

Seven nineteen. Seven plus one is eight plus nine is seventeen. OK.

The closet door swings open. I stumble into the hallway.

"Why not?"

"At a party? Where they auctioned you off like cattle? Christ, Tanya, you used to sell Thin Mints. What happened?" I say.

Somebody bangs on the door. "Hey, Martin! You guys done yet?"

I bang back. "Open the fucking door! Open the fucking door."

The door swings open. I stumble into the hallway.

Dad stands there. "What the—? Where's Kasey?"

"I don't know. I don't know."

A circle of faces peeks in at us, and I crawl out, gulping in the stale party air, the floor sticky-slick with jungle juice.

"What the fuck happened to you, Martin?"

"I don't know. I don't know."

"I don't know."

Dad rushes to the staircase, finding Kasey crumpled like a rag doll at the bottom. He lifts her up, her arm dangling, twisted in an abnormal angle, swollen and blue. "Clean yourself up," he says. "We'll wait in the car."

I change my pants, wash my hands, and put towels over the vomit, piss, and dead rat, my footsteps echoing in the hallway and down the front walk.

I push through the crowd and work my way out front, retching everything in Mario's mom's rosebushes, the thorns scratching at my cheeks.

"Dude, too much to drink, huh?" Some guy's lying on the grass next to a chunky mound of vomit. "Where'd Mario get the spinning grass, man? Home Depot Deluxe? It's a fucking merry-go-round out here. *Wheee-eeee.*" I hear a gurgle and he lies on his side, bilious vomit dripping from his mouth.

Spinning.

Spinning, spinning.

Burning tears spill down my cheeks. I crawl away and hide behind some landscaping boulders, pulling my knees tight to my chest, counting my ragged breaths, making the numbers work so I can clear my head.

I'm supposed to be normal.

My sobs are drowned by the sound of normal that comes from inside the house.

ONE HUNDRED THIRTEEN COMPULSION

Sunday, 2:43 a.m.

Two forty-three. Two times four is eight plus three is eleven. OK.

I flick on the bathroom heater and clutch the toothbrush with stiff fingers.

One, two, three, four, five, six, seven.

Change sides.

Eight, nine, ten, eleven.

Same side.

One, two, three, four, five, six, seven.

Change sides.

Eight, nine, ten, eleven.

I scrape the brush across my tongue until I see blood

spatters in the sink.

Stop.

Stop.

Stop.

Open the cabinet, one, two, three, click closed.

Again.

Again.

My hand trembles. I toss the empty toothpaste in the garbage along with the toothbrush, its bristles splayed out, dotted with brown-red blood. My gums and cheeks sting. My tongue feels like sandpaper, but I gargle the burning mouthwash, holding the liquid in my mouth as long as I can, counting to thirty-seven, then spitting it out, doing it again.

Five times.

I just need to do it five times.

Dad raps on the bathroom door. "Jake, is that you?"

"Uh-huh," I say, almost choking on the mouthwash, the bottle nearly empty now. *One, two, three, four, five . . .*

"Thought you were going to stay at Luc's," Dad says.

Fifteen, sixteen, seventeen, eighteen, nineteen . . . "Uh-uh," I say. Swish, swish, swishing the mouthwash across my teeth, gums, and tongue, getting rid of Tanya's taste. As soon as I'm done here, I'll go to bed. I'll do the numbers, watch a little Bourdain, and wait for sunrise.

Twenty-nine, thirty, thirty-one . . .

That's all I need.

To end right.

Thirty-seven.

Begin right.

New mouthful of wash. Second round. *One, two, three.*

Genesis.

And on the seventh day . . .

"It's pretty late."

"Uh-huh." *Twelve, thirteen, fourteen, fifteen, sixteen, seventeen . . .*

"Good night, then."

"Uh-huh."

Twenty-three, twenty-four, twenty-five, twenty-six, twenty-seven . . . I can hear his breathing outside the door. He pauses.

He should be raging.

I don't look down at my watch because it would fuck up my counting. It's not like I have a curfew. I never go out. But late is late.

It's like he wants to say something.

Maybe I can talk to him.

Swish, swish, swish.

Thirty-two, thirty-three, thirty-four . . .

Maybe I can tell him what's going on; tell him about the numbers and shit. Maybe he'd get it. Maybe he *knows* and is just waiting for me to come clean—like some kind of pop-psychology parent I don't know.

Round three.

One, two, three, four, five . . .

Just a few more swishes and gargles. Two more rounds. Thirty-seven two more times. And I can come out in the hall. We'll sit there. We'll talk.

Before I can finish, he walks away. I hear the soft pad of footsteps walk down the hall. His bedroom door creaks open and clicks shut.

Round four.

Round five.

I spit out the mouthwash, rinsing the sink clean of blood. I stare in the mirror. Everything in my mouth is raw—on fire. The bathroom is clean. Everything's level. The towels are hanging how they need to be, and I open the door with two hands and look down the hallway, waiting for my eyes to adjust to the black night.

No moon tonight.

I finally make out Dad and Mom's door. Closed. No sound comes from their room. I walk to it and lean my ear against it, listening for anything to show me they're awake. A sign to let me know I can go in. We can talk. He can tell me I'm not crazy.

I count to twenty-nine, then to thirty-seven.

Nothing. The silence hurts my ears. I swallow back the knot that has formed in my throat, pinching my nose, trying to keep the burning out.

The salt from my tears burns my lips.

With a trembling hand, I raise my knuckles to knock and remember the look on his face at the game.

Pride.

He was proud.

I relax my fist and wipe the tears off my cheeks. I'm okay. I'm just tired.

Lots going on.

The aura is still here. I need to organize my room before the pain seizes me and I'm out for a few hours. It's not like it always does, but I can't take my chances.

Then everything will be back to normal.

Sunday, 3:21 a.m.

Three twenty-one. Three times two is six plus one is seven. OK.

Just have to bring back the order.

Things were just wrong the last couple of days. Fucked up. Two days leaving before dawn, the other way after.

Leave at dawn.

Because of the sputtering streetlamp—too erratic. Can't be controlled. Gotta call the city to get the light fixed. Then I can leave whenever.

But for now, wake at dawn and go outside.

That's how it works.

I missed it three times in a row.

Wanting it to stop. That was wrong. It's better this way—*my way*. Because it works; it keeps us safe.

I did the routine this morning. We won.

I didn't do it tonight. Everything got fucked up.

It's just a routine. It works. *My normal.*

Five clocks. Two digital. Three analog. I line them up along the windowsill and set them one by one until they're all ticking in unison.

But my favorite watch is the one I wear every day.

I look down at it and make sure it's in time with the five clocks I just set.

Yep.

It was my great-grandpa's. He fought in World War Two and left this vintage military watch to Dad. MIMO SWISS MADE, produced for the German army. When we won our first championship, Dad gave it to me.

I've worn it for three years now. Every day. And it works perfect.

When I remember to wind the fucking thing.

Shit.

Dad says, at least once a week, that the quality of the past can't be matched by the technology of the present. He's big on quality.

Quality.

And he's proud of me.

I slip the watch off and put it on my nightstand, where it always is during the night.

I don't wind it.

I wind on Thursdays and Tuesdays. I wound it on Friday morning, though, because I fucked up.

Tuesday. I'll wind it Tuesday; get back on schedule.

The time is set. Now . . .

. . . call Kase.

Kase. Oh shit. Kase.

Fuck. If I hadn't wanted it to stop, she wouldn't be at the party. When I don't do things the right way, everything spirals out of control.

"I'll be right back, Jakey. Take care of Kasey."

Take care of Kasey.

Fuck.

It's too quiet. I cup my hands over my ears and hear the rumble in my brain, like the roar of the engines before the airplane hurtles down the runway. No screaming. My mind jumps to everything I did wrong since the game and scrambles to put the pieces back together.

So stupid. Stupidstupidstupid. I don't know where to begin.

I was supposed to be normal.

This is normal.

Just. Stop.

Begin again. With the time.

3:27

Three twenty-seven. Good number. Three primes. Three. Two. Seven. Seven plus two is nine plus three is twelve minus seven is five. OK. Two times seven is fourteen plus three is seventeen. OK. Three times two is six plus seven is thirteen. OK.

Exhale. Everything's under control now—now that I'm doing what I'm supposed to. Just as the second hand reaches twelve, I turn my back to the clocks, lying on my left side, facing the door.

I flick open my phone.

Dead.

Fuck.

Where's the charger?

I close my eyes, then turn toward the clocks. I open my left eye, count to three, and watch as the blurry numbers take form. Then I open my right eye.

3:31

Three thirty-one. Three plus three is six plus one is seven. OK. Three minus one is two plus three is five. OK.

My head stops throbbing and the glow of light fades. Things are getting back to normal. Things are working and now everybody's safe. I'm getting the magic.

Three times three is nine minus one is eight minus three is five. OK.

Five-oh-eight and fifty-five—

I slip my left foot out from under the covers and count. One, two, three.

Fifty-six, fifty-seven—

Right foot. One, two, three.

Charger. Need the charger.

I go downstairs and find the charger in the kitchen drawer.

Kaseykaseykaseykaseykasey. Fuck.

Genesis.

The phone beeps when I plug it in.

Seventeen missed calls.

Luc's such an asshole. So I didn't want to get laid. So I'm not like him.

Asshole.

The numbers on the call log are all from Kase.

All seventeen.

One message and one text message:

U @?

Right foot, then left foot, I slide under the covers and listen to the message.

"You told me you'd take me home!" Kase's voice wavers. It's eerily silent in the background and it sounds like she's cupping the phone to her mouth. "You said, 'Got your back.'" The line goes dead.

I call her right back, pressing the phone against my ear, trying to keep the spiders away. "Hello?" a soft voice answers. The reception is shit, crackly.

"Kase? Is that you? What's going on?"

She chokes out a sob. Her words are static; they blur and

run together because of the crap reception.

She's drunk.

"Kase, where's Luc? Where're Kalleres and Grundy?"

What if Kalleres and Grundy ditch her?

What if somebody takes her to a closet?

What if she passes out and asphyxiates in her own vomit?

"Take care of Kasey."

"Mom!" *She's not here. Make the numbers work to keep Kasey and me safe.*

"Take care of Kasey."

"I am. Fuck. What do you think I've been doing all these years with all the fucking numbers? I. Take. Care. Of. Her."

And when I talk, I feel like my mouth is on fire. For an instant, I wonder if I'll choke to death if I fall asleep; if my tongue will fill up my entire mouth and cut off my air.

The crackly line and silence bring me back. Focus. This is about Kasey right now. *She needs me.*

I only hear the sound of candy-wrapper static, then a soft hum of near silence.

"Kase!" I'm holding the phone so tight my knuckles ache. My back feels clammy and my ear doubles with the pressure of the phone.

"Kase!" I can feel the hysteria in my voice. *Keep it together.* "I'll be right there," I say. "Just talk. Let's just talk until I—" The phone clicks off.

I dial again and it kicks me to voice mail right away.

Fuck.

No fucking way. She had to have charged the phone.

I hate batteries.

There should be a kind of windup cell phone. Fucking technology.

I wipe the palms of my hands on the comforter. *One, two, three, four, five. Five, four, three, two, one.*

I'll just get in the car and go to Mario's and pick her up. Not a problem.

Just gotta start the day.

I look at the time and the obsidian sky. It's not dawn. The moonless night falls down onto me, smothering me in blackness.

I try to lift my hand to touch my face, but it lies heavy at my side, as if sticky sap is creeping through my veins, coming to a halt, and my heart races to push the sludge blood through constricted veins. The frenetic beat pounds in my ears. Tingling electrical currents shoot through my body.

I can't move.

Don't leave. Don't leave. Stay here until dawn. Then . . .

Stop. Just stop.

I try to place my hands over my ears—to smother out the frenzied hammering that bangs with every pulse. But I can't move.

I can't move.

I have no control over anything. Nothing.

The sun won't be up until . . .

I force myself to turn to the clock, the digital numbers penetrating the curtain of darkness, giving me light— focus.

Focus.

4:13

Four thirteen. Four plus one is five plus three is eight. Fuck. *Four times one is four times three is twelve.* Fuck.

Think. Think.

The numbers aren't working.

One, two, three, left.

One, two, three, right.

Up.

I push myself out of bed, collapsing to the floor, and move to the door. I turn to the clocks and freeze.

It's wrong.

One of the clocks on the windowsill has stopped.

Go back. Set the time. Get new batteries. Check the others. Just a backup clock, just to get things under control. I go through the closet and pull out the best clocks, ones that won't go dead. This will make it okay. If I do this, then I can go get Kasey.

Okay.

Stop the itching. Stop it. Stop it. Stop it. I cradle my head

between my knees and knead at the back of my neck, pushing down the spiders.

One, two, three, four, five, six. Six clocks.

Six of them.

No. *Five and one.*

I wince but leave them all on the floor, plugging them
into the wall.

*Batteries. Fucking batteries. Zinc-carbon, nickel-cadmium, alkaline
addiction. Okay. Four AA batteries. Easy. Four batteries. Two clocks.
Six. Six. Five and one. Four and two. Four divided by two is two. OK.*

It's okay. Technically it's okay.

Two. OK.

I rifle through my desk drawer for batteries and set the
clocks down in a line on the floor, working them one by
one, until all eleven clocks tick in unison.

Eleven.

Good.

Great number.

It works.

Gotta. Go. She needs help.

I look at my phone. Nothing. No beeps. No messages.
Nothing.

*Maybe we can talk. Just talk. I'll call Grundy. Or Kalleres.
And we'll talk. She'll tell me about her day. We'll wait for dawn
together. It's okay.*

I ring Grundy.

No service. Out of range? Fuck. Did they go to Yosemite or something?

"Can you hear me now? Can your hear me now?"

Dressed. Get dressed.

But I have to start again. Do it right. I get back into bed and stare at the clocks.

4:40

Four forty. Four plus four is eight. Four minus four is zero.

The second hands look like they're all stuck in time. The digital clocks blink, blink, and I concentrate so hard that now it looks like every line glows red or green.

Tick-tock, tick-tock.

I can't see the fucking time.

I squeeze my eyes shut to stop the spinning. My mind feels like a mad merry-go-round whirring and spiraling, chipped paint on metal, hot to the touch, cheeks jiggling, stinging slaps of hair in the eyes, red mouths wide, laughing, laughing, a cyclone of images that shudder to a stop.

But the spinning doesn't stop even when the merry-go-round does.

Everything spins.

Except the North Pole.

Zero miles per hour there.

No spinning. No moving. Nothing to throw me off. No time.

Just night.

Just day.

The North Pole.

The screen on my cell is blank.

ONE HUNDRED THIRTY-ONE WORLD ERASED

Sunday, 4:47 a.m.

Four forty-seven. Four plus four is eight plus seven is fifteen minus four is eleven. OK.

One, two, three, four, five. Elbow, elbow, knee, knee.

I make it to the top of the staircase but have to stop before I retch all over Mom's carpet, before everything goes black.

Call Luc.

I dial him on his cell and am kicked to voice mail. "Hey. I'm not here." *Beep.*

My battery bar is down to two blinking notches. I need to save it . . . just in case.

I get to the hall phone and lean against the wall, whispering in the receiver. *Pick up. Pick up. Fucking pick up the phone.*

"*Hallo?*" a sleepy voice answers. Luc's mom.

I hang up and try to call his cell, but the phone goes *nah-nee-nah*. "We're sorry, but this call cannot be completed as dialed. Please hang up and try again."

Fuck.

Dad had all long-distance and cell phone calls blocked from our house phone unless we punch in a special code because two summers ago Kasey ran up a four hundred–plus–dollar phone bill calling Marcy at summer camp.

I cradle the phone in my hand until I hear the annoying beeps, counting them until I get to fifty-three, then replace the phone in its cradle. I feel better.

Fifty-three.

I crawl to Dad and Mom's bedroom door and lift up my hand to knock. I need to get help. Kasey needs me.

Got your back.

Three words. OK.

"*Take care of Kasey.*"

My stomach churns. I move my ear to the door. Silence. My stomach lurches just thinking about going into that tomblike room.

It's okay.

It's okay. Kasey can wait. Drama queen of the freshman

class can totally wait. I'm sure it's nothing. She probably got in a fight with Marcy.

I block out the other thoughts that work their way through the sticky webs.

I put the phone back on the hook. Kase would find a way to call if she needed something. She'd borrow somebody's phone. She'd really call if she needed me.

But when I search through my message box—now blank—the only thing I can do is curl up into a ball and wait for dawn.

Fifty-three.

I like the way the number forms in my brain and settles, clearing away room for thought.

It's okay.

I can wait.

5:53

The curtain of darkness has receded. I open my left eye, count to three, and watch as the blurry numbers take form. Then I open my right eye.

Five fifty-three. Five plus five is ten plus three is thirteen. OK. Five minus three is two plus five is seven. OK. Five times three is fifteen divided by five is three. OK.

Five fifty-three and fifty-five.

I slip my left foot, as if I were taking it out from under the covers, and count. One, two, three.

Fifty-six, fifty-seven—

Right foot. One, two, three.

Fifty-eight, fifty-nine.

Up.

The hallway is dark—but that's because of the blinds.

I have to be sure there's enough light so that the street-lights don't turn on. So I wait. I can't afford to mess this up.

Kase is counting on me.

I stare at my phone.

Nothing.

It's okay. She's fine. I'll be right there.

What do I need to do? To check?

The clocks. The time.

Okay. It's okay. I'm there.

When it's light enough outside, I go to my room.

I inch toward my bedroom door, grabbing the knob with both hands, opening it until I can see all the clocks lined up.

The watch on my wrist is set in time to the clocks.

And I don't know what to do, which way to go. I concentrate so hard on the numbers, they get blurry. My vision is splotchy.

Turn away. Turn away.

I look back at the clocks that I know are working. What I don't know doesn't count.

6:07

Six-oh-seven. Six plus seven is thirteen. OK. Seven times six is forty-two minus six is thirty-six minus seven is twenty-nine. OK.

The first light of day is already erasing the blackboard night.

I pull on my jeans. Then my left sock, right sock, left shoe, right shoe. My shirt slips over both arms at the same time, perched on top of my head, and I tug it over my face, the soft fabric easing down and settling on my shoulders.

Skip steps eight and four.

At the bottom of the staircase I wait. *I can't afford to forget anything.*

I have to get this right.

I go over the clocks, time, dressing, tooth brushing in my head. Everything is right. No shower. But that's okay. Everything's ready for a shower.

What am I forgetting?

The shrill ring of the phone hurtles me forward—breaks the trance.

Kasey.

Feet pound down the hallway, down the stairs. Dad yanks the Carson Soccer sweatshirt over his head, almost plowing me over. "Move," he says. He pushes his glasses up on his nose. "We've gotta go."

"I'm going. I'm going," I say, my tongue burning with each word. Everything aches—even my teeth.

"What the hell are you doing up?" He pushes past me, and I tap the grandfather clock three times. I manage to open the door with two hands and jump in the passenger side of the car before Dad takes off.

There's no more darkness—only light. Bright November light.

Dad throws the car into reverse and peels out of the driveway, then stops in the middle of the road, the car idling, spewing out billows of black smoke, probably responsible for sixty percent of gas emissions in the state of Nevada.

Dad leans his head on the steering wheel. "Kasey never showed up at Marcy's last night." Dad takes off his glasses and rubs his eyes. Our car blocks the street, and the newspaper delivery van has to veer around us. "Where is Kasey?"

Everything in my mind goes blank, like somebody took a dust mop to the webs and cleared them out, sweeping away the spiders, numbers, leaving me with the image of Kasey alone.

Alone.

And my entire world gets erased.

ONE HUNDRED THIRTY-ONE SORRY

Sunday, 6:09 a.m.

Six-oh-nine. Six times nine is fifty-four minus six is forty-eight . . .

"Just listen to me and what I'm saying."

So rushed. Always in a hurry. I just need to work out—

"Do you know where your sister is?" Dad's breath smells like rancid bacon fat.

Focus . . . forty-eight plus nine is fifty-seven. Fuck.

"Jacob!"

I look at Dad. "She was at Mario's—at a party." I try to put the words together so they'll make sense, my fingers tapping out a prime pattern on the dash. *Two taps, three taps, five taps, seven taps, eleven taps . . .*

"Knock it off," Dad says, pushing my hands off the dash. "How do you know? Did she call you?"

I sit on my hands and swallow the orange-rind taste that covers the back of my tongue. I push the words out. "I. Was. There." Kaseykaseykaseykaseykasey. I stare at the numbers on my watch and can't see them. Blinkblinkblink.

6:11

Six eleven. Six plus one is seven plus one is eight minus one is seven. OK. Six minus one is five divided by one is five. OK.

"You were there? And you *left* her? She's fourteen, for chrissakes, Jacob."

"See. It was supposed to stop. After the win yesterday. They were supposed to go away." He's got to know that. Tears burn my eyes and nose. Spiders crawl up and down, sticky-webbed legs jabbing at my spine.

It was supposed to end. I was supposed to be normal.

He looks at me like he did the day I got stuck in the closet—a curtain of disappointment dusts his features like his real face is breaking through the mask he always wears.

Images and sounds rip through my head, all ending with Kasey screaming for help and me stuck.

Always stuck.

A whole life of numbers, spiders, and lying with no end.

I was supposed to be normal after yesterday's win.

Dad swerves in and out of traffic, just missing a brown Oldsmobile full of gray, wrinkly people. He barrels up

Timberline, half-tread tires spinning on the frosted asphalt as we fishtail up the road, following it until we get to Mario's neighborhood strewn with beer bottles and the vestiges of a five-kegger, two-tub jungle juicer. "Kasey!" I think I'm screaming her name when I tumble out the car door, running up the slippery walk. "Kasey!

"*KaseyKaseyKaseyKaseyKaseKaseKaseK-K-K-K!*" I pound on Mario's door, repeating her name until I lose count and have to start again.

"Stop it." Dad grabs my shoulders. "Look at me."

"*Shhhhhh.* Just *shhhhhh.*" I'm losing count again. "Kaseykaseykaseykaseykasey." A whisper now.

The pain on my cheek is jolting, and the coppery taste of blood fills my mouth. My jaw aches, and I stare at Dad.

"Get your *shit* together, Jacob. We have to find Kasey."

I dial Luc's number. No answer.

Mario opens the door in his jeans, no T-shirt. "Well hello, M&M. Heard you got with Tanya last night. There's *no* wrong way to eat a Reese's, huh?" He wipes the sleep from eyes that get real big when he sees Dad right behind me.

"Where's my daughter?" Dad asks.

Mario looks from my dad to me.

"Is Kasey here?" I look behind his shoulder. "Can you check"—I lower my voice—"the closets?"

"Yeah, man. I'll check. Just a sec." He shuts the door and clicks the deadbolt.

There was no coverage.

Kase's battery died.

I couldn't wake them up.

I had to start the day right.

The lamp sputtered.

Everything makes more sense in my brain, but when I start to say it, I know it's wrong. But how can they understand that this is my fault because of every other day I fucked up? And it wasn't supposed to be like this anymore.

Mario comes back out. "She's not here, man. Sorry," he says.

Dad pushes past Mario and starts hollering Kasey's name.

"Get your old man out of my house," Mario says. He's probably shitting himself that Dad will find his little herb garden. Assmunch.

"Dad?" I say. He doesn't hear me. Nobody does. I don't know if I'm talking or thinking or what the fuck is going on.

Kasey's not here.

Kaseykaseykaseykaseykasey

Dad's cell trills. He listens and loses all color from his face like somebody's erasing him. All I want to do is draw his face back on. *Let them erase me.* This time I know enough to keep my fucking mouth shut.

My fingers begin to itch, scraping across my scalp,

trying to stop the fog and the gray and the numbers. I squat and count the bright drops of blood on the ground, grateful for the throbbing ache in my jaw and nose. Dad's talking. But his words don't make any sense; they're the sound that matches the static, gray in my head.

A car drives up: Luc. He rushes up the porch. "Where's Kasey? What's going on? Jesus, I just woke up and had all these missed calls. Why the fuck didn't you call one of the guys?"

Phrases ricochet off the inside of my skull, bouncing into the trap of silky webs, getting lost into the world of nothingness. I lose the time. I lose the numbers. The only thing I do is repeat her name, willing her to appear.

"At the hospital," Dad says to Luc. The words slice through the gray.

I see her hair—soft brown curls leaning against Dad's shoulder. Her arm twisted, swollen. Blue-black.

I don't know if I'm the one who's screaming or somebody else.

"Sorry. Sorry. Sorry."

One word.

Not OK.

ONE HUNDRED THIRTY-NINE EXPOSED

Sunday, 6:34 a.m.

Six thirty-four. My mind races to work out the numbers.

Dad balls up my sweatshirt front with heavy, callused hands, dry fingertips dusted with fine wood powder. He shakes so hard my teeth clack together. "Not you too. Not you too."

This is not a warning or a plea. It's a statement.

Not me too.

I grasp onto his shoulders to keep from falling back into the evergreen bushes. "I'm so sorry. So sorry."

Sorry. S-O-R-R-Y. Five letters. OK.

Luc places his hand on Dad's shoulder. "Mr. Martin. Please. Stop."

Dad comes back to himself—the anger lifts, and it's just Dad looking at me like he looks at Mom—through me, like the person he thought I was is gone, replaced by whatever it is I have—whatever I am.

But I've always been here. Right. Here.

He's just never chosen to see me. His balled fists release my sweatshirt. I stumble back, and he pulls me up, steadying me, stepping back.

He opens his mouth, then shuts it, looking like a guppy gasping for air when it plops out of a tank. Luc shoves his hands into his pockets and stares at the ground, scuffing his shoes across the frosted sidewalk.

Please. Stop.

How many times did he say that to his dad?

How many times should I have said that to Luc's dad?

Dad clears his throat. "Kasey is at the hospital. So take a breath and get in the car. You've got to get control of this."

What is this? Me?

"I'm right behind you two." Luc opens my door. "C'mon, Jake. C'mon," he urges.

6:41

Six forty-one. Six plus four is ten plus one is eleven.

"Okay." I slump into the car. Luc and I lock eyes through the dew-covered glass. "Okay," I say.

* * *

Each time the doors open, they make this weird whirring sound. People shuffle in and out, quiet except for the whir.

Some carry flowers with them wrapped in soft-colored tissue paper, Crayola-colored stuffed animals, heart-shaped Mylar balloons, cigars wrapped in pink or blue ribbons. Lots of dyed carnations—ripples of petals on thick green stems. Waves. What I imagine ocean waves must look like, each one lapping over the next in a blur of colors.

I can't count the waves.

News travels fast. The waiting room soon crowds with all of Kasey's friends—vodka oozing from everyone's pores. We'll probably get drunk off the fumes.

I look down, readjusting the icepack on my nose and jaw.

A nurse who uses peach-smelling body spritz comes into the room, smothering the sour smell of urine. Some guys from the team walk in and smell up the place as if their pores are Everclear jungle-juice air fresheners. When Kalleres and Grundy walk in, freshly showered with wet hair, reeking tangy, like guilt, I lunge at them, slamming Kalleres against the wall, my fist balled. "You were supposed— Why didn't you call?"

I choke out the words and Luc peels me off Kalleres. "Knock it off, *guevón*."

"Fuck, man," Grundy says. "We're the ones who

brought her here. She's a lightweight."

Kalleres straightens his T-shirt. "She was waiting for you to come back for her."

"Christ, we didn't know she'd get so sick."

"We were just hanging out."

It's like watching Tweedledee and Tweedledum, a Ping-Pong match of assholes. But I'm the one to blame.

I left Kasey.

"I messed up," I say. "It's all my fault."

Luc loosens his grasp on my sweatshirt. "*Guevón*, it's not always about you. Right now, it's about Kasey."

The words hang in the air.

It's about Kasey.

It's about the team.

It's not about me.

What if . . . ?

I shrug Luc off and sit next to Dad. Luc sits next to me. "Just breathe, for fuck's sake," he says.

Tears burn my eyes and nose, and I swallow seven times, then five, then five again, and the fishbowl film of tears that fills my eyes expands until everything in the room is blurry—distorted.

Leaking, leaking, leaking.

Focus.

Focus.

The dam explodes, leaving my cheeks damp, bringing

everything back into focus until the tears well up again.

I stare at my wristwatch, willing the seconds to move faster to catch up to the clock on the wall.

8:23

Eight twenty-three. Eight plus two is ten plus three is thirteen. OK. Eight minus two is six minus three is three. OK. Eight minus three is five plus two is seven. OK.

Eight twenty-three, eight twenty-four. Twenty-three, twenty-four. Two times at the same time like in parallel worlds. I can almost imagine the space before me folding where I can step out and go back or forward by seconds.

"Jake? Jacob!" Dad's voice brings me to the room. I sweep the back of my hand across my eyes, the salt burning my lips. "Stand up. The doctor's here."

The doctor looks tired. "Mr. Martin?" she asks.

"Yes. Yes," he says, holding out a trembling hand.

She shakes Dad's hand—a strong shake, not like a dead-fish shake that lots of chicks do. "I'm Dr. Chen." She looks down at the chart and flips through the pages, then looks back at us. "She's gonna be fine. A pretty lucky young lady, if you ask me. We have some paperwork we need you to fill out before we release her."

The doctor stands there waiting for Dad to respond. His knuckles are white and a blue vein pops out on his forehead.

Dr. Chen's words turn into quiet static. "Pressing

charges . . . Child Protective Services . . . alcohol . . . minors . . ."

I wait. We all do, wondering what will happen.

But nothing else happens.

The doctor stops talking.

She and Dad and the police have come to some kind of agreement that doesn't involve Child Protective Services. The police have already taken everybody's statements and are going on a witch hunt to discover where the alcohol was purchased. Lots of Kasey's friends look really guilty, like they're the ones to blame. They get fidgety and weepy when the cops ask about the booze.

Can't blame them. Who wants to spend four years of high school known as the one who shut down Reed's Highway 50 Mini-Mart? The old man has been selling liquor to minors since Prohibition. He's a Carson landmark.

But really, we all know whose fault this is. I can see it in everybody's eyes—the way they look at me; the murmurs and hushed voices. Or maybe, better put, the way they *don't* look at me.

What if they know about me?

All the work it's taken to keep things hidden. I think about Mera and her dog choking on a chicken bone. Confessions of a vegetarian.

But what am I? What am I confessing?

When the police leave, there's a collective exhale, and I'm sure we'll get carbon dioxide poisoning. I'm just glad there's a fern in the waiting room and I move toward it, counting the fronds.

The morning almost feels scripted: a gathering of our closest friends, Kasey's imminent danger, my total impotence in more ways than I'd care to admit, and the inevitable awkward silence while everybody either looks at me or avoids looking at me.

What if they know about me?

What if . . . ?

I try to piece together the idea of what it will be like now that everybody knows the truth—the truth about me. But I don't even know what that is. I just know I'm not right, somehow.

What if . . . ?

People trickle out of the hospital, throwing around phrases like *one lucky girl* and *intense morning*, reliving everything like they were the ones who found her—who saved her. And I'm the one who left her for dead. They slip away so they won't have to look at me anymore, and I feel like a Scooby-Doo villain whose fictitious face has been peeled off to expose the real me. The real me has leaked out over the floor in goopy puddles. There's nowhere to hide.

Dad tugs on my sweatshirt and says, "Quit fidgeting."

8:27

Eight twenty-seven. Eight plus two is ten plus seven is seventeen. OK.

"What is your problem, Jacob?" Dad wrenches my face around until we're practically nose to nose. He lowers his voice. "You need to get your act together. Now."

"C'mon, man." Luc pushes me behind Dad and the doctor. "I'll come by later to check up on things at the Martins'."

Luc smells worse than he looks. "Get some sleep," I say. "And a shower."

"Will do." He doesn't laugh like he's supposed to. He's not acting the part. He pauses, caterpillar eyebrows scrunched together. His frame is silhouetted against the waiting-room window—bright sunlight streams in and hurts my eyes. I'm stuck here again—stuck in the door between inside and outside, between perception and reality, truth and lies.

Kasey is lying on a bed behind a seafoam-green curtain—the metal rings sliding across the bar making a *swish-swish* sound. Kasey looks tiny, sandwiched between monitors. A blue-black bruise has formed on her cheek.

"Hey," I say.

"Not. So. Loud," she whispers. "Where's my stuff?"

A nurse hands her a paper bag of clothes. Kasey looks in, takes a whiff, and says, "Could you not have brought me fresh clothes?"

"We didn't think about it."

She glares at me. "A little privacy, please."

"Oh. Yeah." I pull the curtain shut and wait in the cramped hallway. "Kase, are you okay?"

"Where's Mom?" she asks through the curtain.

"At home. She's sick." I sound like Dad.

"Mom should be here. Moms come to hospitals when their kids are sick."

"Kase—" I say.

"Mom's *never* here. What's your excuse?"

"What do you mean?"

"You bailed on me. You *left* me."

"I'm here now."

"A lot of good that does."

Then silence.

Some guy lies still on a gurney down the hall, attached to a heart monitor, a tube shoved down his throat, filling him up with air.

I hate the sound of the beep of the heart monitor and the hum of the oxygen that fills his lungs—in and out, in and out. It's a grating, choking sound; it's artificial and cold. And after each lung filling it clicks, then air whooshes out, and the machine begins to fill him up again.

Noisy. Quiet places are the noisiest.

The little needle of green light jigs up and down. Blood pressure 90 over 60, 87 over 63, the numbers click and change in front of me and my mind races to keep up.

The numbers come with certain clarity, organizing my mind, bringing things back from chaos to order. I go from the pulse number to blood pressure, count the lines and crags in the regular beating of the guy's heart, swallowing back the anger and regret.

Regret.

That pretty much wraps up everything about who I am.

ONE HUNDRED FORTY-NINE BREAKING NORMAL

Sunday, 9:31 a.m.

Nine thirty-one. Nine plus three is twelve plus one is thirteen. OK.

I fidget with my watch and bring it to my ear, listening to the soft tick. *Tick-tock. Tick-tock.*

We sit in deafening silence on the way home, waiting for the explosion; the heat radiating from Dad's body has to do major ozone damage.

"I don't know what the matter is with you. Either of you." He looks at me when he talks, though. I'm the problem. I know this.

Not you too.

"Drink water. Get some sleep," he says to Kasey, and

goes into the garage after putting out some snack food.

Kasey takes a twenty-three–minute shower, totally breaking Dad's five-minute rule, comes downstairs, and crumples on the couch. Mom leaves the bedroom a couple of times to check on us from the top of the stairs, then retreats to the safety of her four walls.

"I have to tell you about last night," I whisper.

Kasey doesn't move.

"I have to tell you now. Like this. Until I can figure out a way to, I don't know, *really* tell." The words fill the room, and I'm afraid they'll get engraved in the walls. But they don't. They disappear as soon as I say them. It's like practice. Because I have to tell somebody—sometime. It's hard to know how to tell something I don't even understand myself.

I just need a sign.

So I stare at the grandfather clock, work out the numbers, and try to figure out where they're trying to steer me. Who can I tell?

"What happened to your face?" Kase taps me on the shoulder, jerking my attention from the clock.

"Hey," I say, rubbing my eyes. "Want me to get Dad? Do you need something?"

"No thanks. He still pissed?"

"He hasn't left the garage since we came home."

"Yikes. Major Doritos Smokin' Cheddar Barbecue?"

"More like Atomic Ass-Blaster Hot Habañero."

"That's not a real flavor."

"Well, it should be."

"So what happened to your face?" Kasey leans in and pulls my chin close to hers. "And your mouth?"

"Nothing," I say.

"'Ethel Thayer, thounds like I'm lithping, doethn't it?'"

"Ha. Ha."

"Well, you look like shit and talk like a testosterone-heavy Daffy Duck. Well, not *that* heavy, according to party gossip."

"Yeah. Well—"

"Well what?" There's an edge to her voice.

"I'm sorry. I'm sorry I bailed."

"Sorry. That does a lot of good, doesn't it?"

"I'm not saying it does."

"So why are you even saying it at all?"

"What else can I say?"

"The million-dollar question."

She motions to the plate of cheese and crackers Dad left covered with Saran wrap on the table. I pass her the plate and she places a slice of cheese on top of each cracker, puzzle-piecing it together so the entire cracker face is covered and no cheese hangs over the sides.

"Kase," I say, "you called last night and—"

She eats her crackers outside-in until she only has a little center to pop on her mouth. "And what?" she says through bites.

"Did anybody take you to the closets? At Mario's?" The thought sends searing pain through my nerves. I squeeze my head between my knees, half hoping my eardrums will blow and I'll go deaf and won't have to hear what happened to Kasey at Mario's.

I am such a coward.

I sit up and stare her in the eyes. "Did something happen?"

By now she's finished her crackers and has peeled a bunch of grapes.

Who the fuck peels grapes?

"Did something happen, you ask. Yeah. I got as much action last night as you did."

"You're just tearing it up, Kase. Can you get real for second?"

"What do you expect me to say? You're the one who comes off as being gallant, shy, the quirky soccer star that respects *Reese*? C'mon."

"Kasey—"

She holds up her hand. "Don't. My entire social life blew up last night when I puked on your soccer friends and blacked out, only to have moments of pseudoconsciousness listening to Kalleres repeat himself over and again, 'Dude, what are we s'posed to do? Dude?' Are those guys even literate? And why do you all insist on calling each other *dude*?" She peels another grape, taking out the seeds and popping it in her mouth.

"Then to make matters worse, they drag me around the party until somebody agrees to give us a ride to the emergency room, but, once again, *only* because I'm *your* baby sister. So now I will be officially known as Jacob Martin Superhero's puking baby sister. You know what they're gonna call me? Earl. Fish feeder. Technicolor yawn. Fergler. There will be no end. I'll be voted Most Likely to Marry a Guy Named Ralph. It's over for me. Totally over."

Kase is more preoccupied with her impending fall from the social hierarchy than the fact that she'll be grounded until she's twenty-one which, in and of itself, will pretty much squelch any kind of social life she strove to have in the first place.

"All right. All right," I say, holding up my hands. "But—"

"But what?"

"Why do you care so much about them?"

"Who's them?"

"I dunno who they are: the higher echelon of Carson High's social circles. Why do they—this nondescript *they*—matter?"

"It's easy for you to say, Mr. UCLA, Maryland, wherever-you're-gonna-go-and-be-famous," she says. "You never step outside of yourself for a second. It's like the world that you live in is perfect and everybody else lets you be there. Everything's easier for you because of who you are. And harder for me because of who you are."

A thick crease forms between Kase's eyebrows. "I'm *not* gonna be the girl who doesn't get invited to any parties in high school—you know, the one who doesn't even know about them until the Monday after."

"I don't go to parties," I interrupt.

"Yeah. But that's because you don't *want* to. You're always invited."

I sigh.

"What about your day? Do you want to tell me about it?"

Kase shrugs. "I was picked up from the hospital by my dad and brother. The latter totally humiliated me in front of all of Carson High and possibly the only guy who will ever want to hook up with me, then bailed—and my crazy mom hasn't even bothered to see if I'm all right."

"Kase, that's mean. Mom's worried."

"Yeah. Real worried. Worried she hit an imaginary bicyclist with an imaginary car or stole imaginary groceries from some guy seven weeks ago. Sure, she's worried. She's just not worried her only daughter could've died or been drugged and gotten raped at a party."

Not you too. Dad's words keep tapping on my brain. But I don't do the same shit Mom does. We're not even on the same playing field. I stare at Kasey's grape peels and the seeds on her plate—all lined up in perfect symmetry.

Are we okay?

"Kase, it's not like that. *You're* not like that."

"Then what is it like?" she asks. "What? Should I put a Band-Aid on it like we always do around here?" She rolls her eyes. "Oh, c'mon. Don't do that *Sesame Street* stuff with me. I know who I am. And I know what I want other people to think I am. That's the game, isn't it?" Kasey brushes invisible crumbs off her lap into her cupped hand and piles them on her plate.

Perception. Reality. I wonder what it would be like to peel off my skin and become the person everybody else sees—or wants to see. Just for a day. Just for an hour. That Jake must be pretty amazing.

We sit in silence for a while until I say, "It's a shitty game."

"We all play it."

"Wouldn't it be easier just to be real for once?"

Kase swallows her last grape. "I don't know anybody who is and survives high school."

I think about Mera. She's surviving. But she might have a volleyball named Wilson she talks to in order to refrain from hurling herself off the top of the Empire State Building.

"I just want her to be a mom, you know? Sometimes I just want a mom."

I get that. I don't remember the last time we had one.

"You think I'll be grounded?" Kase asks.

"Yeah. We both are."

"Until when?"

"I think until we can go to federal prison—so I only have about ten months left. You've got three years."

"Funny."

"Dad's already looking into getting those house-arrest anklets. They're all the rage."

Kase tries to stay stone-faced. "Real funny." She glances up the staircase.

"She's checked on you a couple of times."

"And that's supposed to make me feel better?"

"No. I guess not. But it's something."

"That's all we get? Something."

"I think that's all we get."

"What if it's not good enough?"

I scratch my watch face, rubbing off something sticky. Kase looks so small right now, like when she used to bring art projects home in elementary school. I wrap my arm around her shoulders, then give her the biggest big-brother bear hug I can muster. She wipes her eyes and rubs guck off my shoulder.

I think about Mom and me—and for the very first time I wonder if Kase is sick, too: the cleaning, food symmetry, always keeping everything in order. Does she feel as desperate as I do?

It's not just about me anymore.

It never has been.

"Can you just tell me about your day?" And this time I'm asking for her, not for me. She sits with her legs crossed and I sit facing her, knee-to-knee.

And I listen.

Sunday, 5:23 p.m.

Five twenty-three. Five times two is ten plus three is thirteen. OK.

There's a shuffle and murmur of voices outside the door. Dad peeks his head in, his face lighting up when he sees Kasey. "Look remorseful," I whisper.

Dad tries to put his angry face back on, but I can tell he's just happy to see her, happy she's here. He walks to the couch and sits next to her. She hugs him like it's the easiest thing to do in the world. He kisses the crown of her head. I feel like an invader sitting here, so I remain still, trying to become invisible. I scan the room until I focus on the numbers of the microwave clock, feeling the rush of relief as my brain kicks back into motion, settling down the knot of anxiety that has balled up in my stomach.

I look up to see Luc standing in the garage door.

"Why don't you and Luc go outside and talk," Dad says. "Then I think you and I have a few things to discuss."

Even though having Dad know everything terrible about me is horrifying, I feel lighter somehow, like all the numbers and calculations that have weighed me down so long can be shared with somebody.

But something itches in the back of my mind. *Not you too.*

I nod at Dad. "I will." And I follow Luc outside onto the porch.

I stay under the eaves, my legs tucked under me so I'm not technically outside. So I don't have to touch the flamingo before going back in. Luc tosses me a CD. "This was in your mailbox. Your dad said it had to be yours."

I hold the CD in my hands. *Bolero.* "Thanks."

"What is it?"

I show him.

"Classical stuff?"

"Yeah."

"That's cool." Luc hands me an ice-cold can of Coke. "Thought you could use some company."

"Did my dad ask you to come?" I ask.

"No, *guevón.* You're my friend." He looks at me like I'm

Idiot Jake, not Crazy Jake.

"Oh. Thanks."

I pop open the Coke, listening to the fizz, feeling the spray, drinking the first sips too fast and ending up with a nasty case of the hiccups. The hiccups stop after I get to fifty-eight.

Fifty-eight. Five plus eight is thirteen. OK.

Eight minus five is three. OK.

"Thanks for the Coke. Add it to my bill."

"Nah. This one's on me." He taps his fingers on the top of his Coke can and pulls back the tab.

"Thanks," I repeat, and stare at the time.

5:27

Five twenty-seven. Five minus two is three plus seven is ten divided by two is five. OK.

Stop.

Stop.

Stop.

I dig my nails into my palms and squeeze until half-moons are embedded in my hands. I scrape my nails across my hands, pulling me away from the numbers, back to Luc. He sips on his Coke, leaning forward with his elbows on his knees. He nods toward the house. "She's okay, right? Like nothing weird went on last night."

"Nothing weird. I guess her blood alcohol content was something like point two three—insanely high."

"*Mierda*. That's one hangover."

"Yeah. All she's done half the day is sleep, moan, roll over, and go back to sleep."

Point two three. Three plus two is five. OK.

We sit in silence. Luc doesn't even try to talk to me about the game or anything. That's good. I don't have the energy to pretend today. We watch the street. Silence. But a comfortable kind of silence that makes me glad Luc's my friend.

It's getting cold. Luc stands up. "Better head home. I haven't even touched my homework; Juancho's working on some engine and wants my help."

"You like that?" I ask. "Working on cars."

Luc pauses, like he's never been asked that before. And I realize that it goes both ways—the asking stuff. He nods. "I do. I'm good at it. You know, it's nice to be good at something." He gives me a half hug and claps me on the back. "Come by. You can check out my work."

"Will do," I say. "Maybe you can teach me how to change the oil or something."

"That coming from the guy who's driven a total of three times since he turned sixteen? You probably better stick to learning how to drive first. I'll be your family mechanic."

I laugh. "Fair enough."

Luc looks back at the house. "She's kinda like my baby sister too." He steps out into the yard, standing next to the pink flamingo. His fingers brush the beak.

"You need to come inside?" I ask. "It's cold."

He touched the beak. He has to come in.

Stop. It.

"Nah, man. I've really gotta go."

Let. It. Go.

My fingers burn—like they're the ones that touched the beak—urging me inside. I stare at the tips, waiting for blisters to form.

Luc's halfway down the walk when I look up from my fingers. *How come he doesn't need to come in when he touches it?*

"Hey, Luc," I call after him.

"Yeah?" he says.

"You're not him, you know."

"Who?"

"Your dad. You're not even close."

Luc crunches the Coke can in his fist. "Yeah. Maybe."

"Absolutely," I say.

"Thanks," Luc says. He looks relieved. "I needed to hear that, you know. That's good to hear."

I nod. "Are you okay?" I ask.

Luc lets the question sink in. He jingles his car keys. "Yeah. I'm okay."

And I believe him.

Sunday, 6:13 p.m.

Six thirteen. Six plus one is seven plus three is ten times six is sixty plus one is sixty-one. OK.

Kasey's gone to her room. Mom's asleep. Dad's sander buzzes in the garage.

I pull out a frozen dinner and pop it into the toaster oven, watching the heating element turn crimson, feeling the heat on the door. The kitchen clock ticks as the second hand works its way around the circle, and I like the way time is circular; the beginning is the end.

The timer *ding*s and I pull out the steaming plate of roast beef, fake potatoes, and sludge-brown gravy. It all tastes like cardboard, but I'm hungry, so I eat, tapping my foot whenever the second hand hits a prime.

I throw the plate in the garbage. A thousand years from now a scientist will know what I had for dinner on November 6. And maybe they'll have the technology to study my DNA and figure out why I was a mutant. Why I am the way I am.

I sit at the base of the steps and wait.

And count.

I don't even try to keep the webs from crowding my brain, because maybe Dad and I can figure things out together. I'm just so tired of doing it all alone.

Dad's sander dies down. I listen to the soft brush of the broom across the garage floor. He walks in the door, flicking on the light. "Jacob!" He jumps. "Why are you sitting in the dark like this?"

"I dunno," I say. I didn't even notice the dark. It just felt good to be invisible, I guess.

Dad pours himself a drink from a dusty bottle tucked behind the cabinet. He plops two ice cubes in and swirls the drink around the glass, making a whistling sound, taking a sip, bracing his body for the burning liquid. He comes and sits next to me on the staircase. "Jacob, about this morning—"

"I know," I say. "I know. I just couldn't—" I'm trying to find the words to describe everything that happened this morning to make it sound right. *Sane.* "I'm sorry."

Dad puts his hand on my shoulder and squeezes, shaking his head. "You've had to grow up quick, take a lot of responsibility. I know it's a burden."

He knows.

Not you too.

I brush it off. He'll be okay with it. He has to be. He's my dad. That's why we're talking. He *wants* to know.

I just hope I can say what's real.

"All that hiding. All that trying to be something that—" Dad looks at me and I don't look away. I open my mouth, but I'm not sure what I should say. Where should I begin? When did it begin? It's hard to imagine what will come out when I've been saying the other script—the "right" words—for so long.

A draft comes from under the door. It's cold. I shiver and go to the hall closet to pull out my coat. The door swings and clicks shut behind me, enclosing me in blackness except for the green light of my Indiglo watch. The doorknob is jammed.

There's a snap and the sickening sound of bones breaking—the rat's chest rises and falls, then shudders. It whines out its last breath, the trap shoved between a rubbery Halloween clown mask with bulging eyes and a rubbery winter boot.

Silence.

Waiting for Mom, listening to Kasey's screams.

Waiting, counting, staring at the Indiglo watch face, trying to clear my brain because I know if I don't, I'll die.

Tick-tock, tick-tock.

The numbers keep me alive. Keep Kasey alive. Just count. Make the numbers work.

Tick-tock, tick-tock. . . .

Yesterday, it was supposed to end.

Magic number three.

My feet remain glued to that spot—that moment. It's like being chased in a dream, leaden legs pushing through thick tar, and just as soon as I move away, something snaps me back to the place where the spiders will get me.

Tick-tock, tick-tock.

"Your mother just isn't well. I can't understand it, because she's fine. But she's not. It's so—"

I pause. "Mom." *What about me?*

"With overtime at work and taking carpentry orders for Christmas, I'm going to need you to be prepared to take on more responsibility around the house. We need the money." He rubs his hands together, making a scratchy sound from the rough calluses on his palms. "It's not fair. I know. But with your mom sick . . . "

"What is it?" I ask. "What does she have?" I want the

name. At least give me the name for it.

Dad shakes his head. "I don't understand it. It's almost like she's a child sometimes. And I can't remember how we got to where we are right now. I used to think it was cute we'd have to drive back to the house to make sure everything was turned off. And she'd save all the receipts—of groceries that we'd bought the year before. And your presents. She still has a box of receipts of everything she ever bought for you and Kasey, just to make sure."

"To make sure what?"

Dad stares into his drink, like it can offer the answers. "It doesn't make sense. I don't understand why—" Dad finishes his drink. "It doesn't matter, I guess. We just have to work through this until she bounces back."

I shake my head. "It's okay, Dad. I'll take care of things."

"We're okay, then." He says it like it's an irrefutable fact. We. Are. Okay. "I'm counting on you."

Counting.

I can hear my voice sounding strong, steady, while everything inside feels like it's melting. "Dad, is there anything I can do?"

"It's been a long day. Tomorrow will be better."

I rub my temples, trying to calm the dull pounding inside my brain. I just have to get through the day. *Tomorrow will be better.*

But somehow I know that tomorrow will be just like

today and yesterday.

I'm so tired of the same.

Dad ruffles my hair. "Jacob, I'm proud of you. Do what you love. Keep playing soccer, go to the best college you can, get a degree. After this year, it's your time. I promise to never ask the impossible from you again."

He doesn't get it.

He just did.

ONE HUNDRED SIXTY-THREE NIGHT WHISPERS

Monday, 3:14 a.m.

Three fourteen. Three plus one is four plus four is eight minus three is five. OK.

Everybody sleeps.

That's what everybody's supposed to do at night. Sleep.

The numbers rip through my head.

I can hear the *drip, drip, drip* of the kitchen sink faucet. *Drip, drip, drip, dri-ip.* At first it sounded like cymbals, softly tapping together. Now the sound is muffled, deep, and the drips thud into a puddle of water.

The wind rustles the trees outside and whistles in through the broken downstairs window.

Whistle, drip, whistle, drip.

I count them.

Fuck.

I put in my earphones and crank up *Bolero*, trying to push away the sounds of the night—of the house. The melody gets louder and louder but the steady beat behind it traps the melody in the song. *Dum dadadadadada dum dada dum; dah dadadadadadada* . . .

I hate this song.

I rip the earphones out and stare at the clock.

3:17

Three seventeen. Three plus one is four plus seven is eleven. OK. Seven minus three is four minus one is three. OK.

I turn over in bed.

Drip, drip, drip, dri-ip. Whistle, drip, whistle, drip. Thud.

3:19

Three nineteen. Three plus one is four plus nine is thirteen. OK.

I slip my left foot out from under the covers and count. *One, two, three.*

Fifty-six, fifty-seven—

Right foot. One, two, three.

Fifty-eight, fifty-nine.

Up.

I slip downstairs and freeze when I see Dad. But I can't go back upstairs until I fix the drip, so it's like I'm stuck in syrup, like those bugs they find in tree sap thousands of years later. I'm frozen in time like a prehistoric mosquito.

Dad sits at the dining room table, bills splayed on the table in a fan of red overdue notices. He tidies papers into small piles, then pauses, like he's forgotten what he's supposed to be doing, then tidies more, piling again, re-organizing, taking papers off, finally leaning back against the chair and closing his eyes. He doesn't see me see him.

I step forward and put my arm on his forearm. "Dad," I say, and search for the right words. "It's okay," I whisper. His rough hand slips into mine.

ONE BEGINNING

Monday, 4:31 a.m.

Four thirty-one. Four plus three is seven plus one is eight divided by four is two. OK.

What would it be like to be real? Just once. Even just for one morning?

There's a Bourdain marathon on. He's eaten his way through half of the Middle East and is now at some state fair in Georgia bingeing on deep-fried Oreos, pickles, Coca-Cola, and Cadbury Creme Eggs. Tanya would probably gain weight just watching it.

I wonder if Bourdain has some special kind of health plan that won't cover artery damage.

I wonder if Mera is watching.

The light sputters outside. I can see the flicker on my curtains. *Sputter, sputter.* I don't hold my breath and stand up, getting out of bed. My body feels clammy. I fight nausea and turn my back from the window, pulling on my clothes and then stepping into the hallway.

The metallic taste of blood fills my mouth. I realize I'm gnawing on my raw cheeks, breaking the blistered skin.

Stop.

What if . . .

Nothing happens. Nothing changes. The house still sleeps even though I'm up before dawn and haven't held my breath, waiting for the sputtering to end.

Nothing changes.

Just like in *Bolero.*

Maybe that's what it's all about—setting the limits and sticking to them, no matter how much you want to scream.

That's what I've always done. I thought there was an end to forever. Saturday was supposed to end it. It didn't work.

Since I don't eat like Bourdain, I probably will live till I'm eighty or ninety.

Forever's a long time.

Getting to the top of the staircase is like trying to walk through drying concrete. *How is it that I can't just do a simple thing?*

Leave before dawn.

Just leave.

I push myself downstairs, skipping eight, then four. I step on the bottom stair, and it sends a deafening shriek through the house.

Nobody stirs.

A soft clicking noise comes from the heater, followed by a *whooshing* sound of air being piped into the rooms.

Outside, the inky sky is painted a black so thick, stars can't even shine through.

I'll wait. Until dawn. Then it'll . . .

It'll be the same tomorrow and the next day and the next day . . .

Forever's a long time.

I tap the grandfather clock, open the door with two hands, and step outside into a couple inches of snow. The flamingo is dusted with a layer of powdered-sugar snow. I'm glad I don't have to touch the beak, marring the perfect coat.

I count my steps.

Eight hundred fifty-seven. Eight plus five is thirteen plus seven is twenty minus eight is twelve minus seven is five. OK.
4:53 a.m.

Four fifty-three. Four plus five is nine plus three is twelve minus five is seven. OK.

The second hand works its way around the watch, but for some reason the second hand does this weird pause when

294

it hits forty-seven seconds. I tap the watch, shake it, but the second hand pauses.

This is wrong. All wrong.

Light floods the driveway for a third time. Time ticks ahead. 4:54. 4:55.

I stand in the shadows, then move forward.

4:56

I try to time my steps. *Four fifty-six. Four plus five is nine plus six is fifteen minus four is eleven. OK.*

It's perfect. It's time.

I walk up to the front door and look down at my watch. *Four fifty-seven.* The numbers don't work. *Sixteen. Eight. Nine.* I can feel the tension creep up the back of my head and extend its tentacles, releasing fire ants in my nerves. The pain seizes me and, again, I'm stuck in the shadows between the numbers.

Darkness sweeps across my eyes like a veil. The door looks blotchy, but I move forward, holding my hand out to ring the bell.

5:01

Five-oh-one. Five plus one is six. Five minus one is four. Not OK. OK.

"Jacob Martin?" The door swings open. Mera's dad stoops down to pick up the newspaper. "What the hell are you doing here at this time of day?"

I stare at my shoes—the laces tied, double-knotted.

"Can I see Mera, please?" I can't imagine he can hear me above the percussion pounding of my heart. "Is Mera here?" I repeat.

"Son, I'm not deaf. Mera!" he hollers down the hallway. "Jacob Martin is here." His tone softens. "About the other day at the shop—"

I can see lawsuit written all over his words. I want to tell him the damage was done long ago, though, so not to worry. I hold up my hand. I can hardly hear him through the pulsing arteries in my brain. "It's okay, Mr. Hartman." Just a whisper now. "It's okay."

Mera comes to the door and stands next to her dad. "Thanks, Dad." She's wearing flannel pajama bottoms and a heavy sweatshirt. "Do you want to come in?" she asks. "It's pretty cold out there." Her words come out with puffy white breaths, circling us, then swirling up to the blackness.

I shake my head, cradling it between my hands, trying to stop the pain. I sit down on the porch steps, wet snow seeping through my jeans.

Mera leaves and returns, draping a blanket over my shoulders. She sits next to me on the porch, smelling like sleep and warm gingerbread.

Inhale.

Exhale.

Inhale.

I listen to her get up, go inside, and come back out. A

ACKNOWLEDGMENTS

I am so grateful for:

An amazing team at HarperCollins that works so hard doing a million things to make my books the best they can and make sure my books get out there: Cindy Hamilton, Renée Cafiero, Emilie Ziemer, Laura Lutz, and Jenny Rozbruch.

My first publisher, Laura Geringer, who took a chance on me, and my current publishers, Alessandra Balzer and Donna Bray, who continue to believe in my work.

My amazing editor, Ruta Rimas, who knows how to ask the right questions, pushing me to my limits as a writer.

My out-of-this-universe agent, who trusts in my crazy notions, somehow knowing that those vague ideas in my head can become novels.

My critique group and family who believed before I did.

Finally, this book would be nowhere without Lisa. She trusted me with her stories. She took a risk, sharing her world with me, and without her help, I would never have been able to imagine Jake.

Mental illness, of any kind, is commonly misdiagnosed, ignored; and those who suffer often suffer alone. I hope that this book, in some way, will open a door and maybe give someone who does suffer the courage to come forward. You are not alone.

comfortable silence surrounds us. I pull my head up, waiting for my eyes to focus.

She passes me a hot cup of cocoa. "Soy cocoa," she says. "Soy is better for you than regular cow milk. Marshmallows." She drops in a handful. "*Not* organic. Organic marshmallows taste like compost."

I cradle the cup in my hands. Eight marshmallows. I flick one out.

Seven. OK.

"Are you okay?" She links her arm with mine.

The acid bubbles from my stomach, leaving a nasty film in my mouth. I sip on the cocoa, the hot liquid burning my throat, melting through the ice that has formed there, leaving me mute all these years. The spiders spin and weave their webs through every nerve, squeezing, crunching, reminding me I did everything wrong this morning.

Everything is wrong.

Everything has been wrong for a long time. But I don't know how this can make it any better.

"Are you okay?" she repeats.

The words form in my brain, breaking through the fog, slipping through the silky webs. I cup Mera's hand in mine, swallowing again.

"I don't think so."